"I saw that panicked look on your face when I was sitting with Riley. You looked like I was fixin' to scare the poor kid."

"I knew from experience that the more you push a boy that age, the further you push him away," Tyler said.

Beth heard the pain in his voice. "You've been there and done that."

"I ran through five foster care homes in two years. I was known as a troublemaker until I got to the Olaskys. They didn't ask me to open up. They gave me the room and the respect I needed." He gave a soft laugh. "But I got toted to church and that's where the Lord got a hold of me. After that, I was willing to talk."

"Well, I hope we made a breakthrough with Riley."

"We'll see."

Beth took a deep breath. Tyler had revealed another layer of himself and her heart whispered he was a good man. He'd slipped past the shield she'd erected around her heart. And oddly enough, that realization didn't panic her.

Books by Leann Harris

Love Inspired

Second Chance Ranch
Redemption Ranch

Love Inspired Suspense

Hidden Deception
Guarded Secrets

LEANN HARRIS

When Leann Harris was first introduced to her husband in college she knew she would never date the man. He was a graduate student getting a PhD in physics, and Leann had purposely taken a second year of biology in high school to avoid taking physics. So much for first impressions. They have been married thirty-eight years and still approach life from very different angles.

After graduating from the University of Texas at Austin, Leann taught math and science to deaf high school students for a couple of years until the birth of her first child. When her youngest child started school, Leann decided to fulfill a lifelong dream and began writing.

She is a founding member and former president of the Dallas Area Romance Writers. Leann lives in Dallas, Texas, with her husband. Visit her at her website, www.leannharris.com.

Redemption Ranch
Leann Harris

Love Inspired

Recycling programs for this product may not exist in your area.

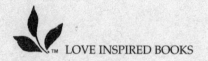

LOVE INSPIRED BOOKS

ISBN-13: 978-0-373-81615-6

REDEMPTION RANCH

Copyright © 2012 by Barbara M. Harrison

www.LoveInspiredBooks.com

Printed in U.S.A.

Therefore, there is now no condemnation
for those who are in Christ Jesus.
—*Romans* 8:1

To my wonderful husband, the computer guru
who keeps me up and running.

Chapter One

"Oh, Charming, what's wrong with me?" Beth McClure ran her hands down the gelding's broad back. His warm coat and steady heartbeat calmed her.

Twenty minutes ago her brother and his wife, her best friend and former college roommate, had announced there would be a new McClure come spring. Friends and family gathered at the ranch cheered the news.

Beth was glad for them, really.

And sad.

It was selfish of her, but the news stabbed her in the heart, making her realize how alone she was. Oh, sure, she had family, friends, but there was not a prospect of a boyfriend in sight. In some ways she was content to be alone, but her heart still ached.

Charming raised his head and stepped back,

knocking Beth into the back wall of the stall. She stumbled, her skirt tangling in her legs, and she twisted her ankle. Wearing heels out in the stables wasn't smart, but she wasn't worrying about that when she escaped.

"Charming, what's wrong with you?" She pushed the horse away as she searched for her shoe. Charming danced again, bumping her a second time. She fell against the side of the stall, losing her other shoe.

"Stop." She glanced over her shoulder to see what was making the horse so nervous. She spotted the black dog sitting outside the open stall door.

"Oh, sorry, guy." Beth patted Charming on his back hip to quiet him. The black dog sat quietly, watching her. Beth recognized him. He belonged to the newest employee of Second Chance Ranch, Tyler Lynch. He was an Iraqi War veteran like her brother Zach. Tyler's dog, Dogger, was known as a cautious critter who didn't offer his friendship lightly, much like his owner. In the month Tyler had been at the equine therapy ranch, she'd never known his dog to allow anyone to pet him, and she only had a nodding acquaintance with the dog's owner.

Tyler would politely nod his head or keep up his end of a conversation, but he'd subtly let a person know there was a wall between him and the world. Beth knew that "look." Zach had worn the exact same expression when he came home from his tour of service.

Intrigued, Beth moved to the front of the stall. "Hey, guy, how are you?"

The dog cocked his head. He had the look of a mutt, short dark hair, mid-size, sleek and with white stockings on his back feet. He had a half-moon scar on the back of his head.

"Are you declaring a truce?" she asked, inching forward.

Charming stretched his neck down toward the dog. Beth reached under the horse's neck and patted the other side. "What do you think, big guy? You think he wants to make friends?" She whispered the question out of the side of her mouth.

The horse raised his head and nodded.

Beth's hand fell to her side. "You want me to pet you?" she asked, directing her question to the dog.

Dogger looked from Charming to Beth as if considering the question.

Beth laughed. She stepped out of the stall and held out her hand. The dog moved toward her and sniffed. He sat, waiting for her to oblige him.

Beth squatted and stroked the dog's head. He accepted her affection. She'd tried to make friends with the dog a couple of times before, but he'd refused her overtures.

"You're a mighty cagey boy. Did you decide to watch and wait to make sure I was worthy of your trust?"

The dog closed his eyes, enjoying the petting.

"Well, I be—"

Beth jerked at the sound of Tyler's voice, losing her balance. She sprawled onto the floor, her skirt drifting gracefully around her knees.

"Sorry." The corner of Tyler's mouth twitched, making that hands-off look he normally wore melt away. Her stomach dipped.

It was nothing but embarrassment, she told herself as she looked up from the floor into his handsome face. "You startled me."

He offered his hand.

There was no dignified way to get to her feet. She accepted his hand and he pulled her to her feet. Beth dusted off hay from the backside of her skirt. The laugh trying to escape her chest erupted. "You must think I'm a klutz."

"No," he said, his eyes twinkling.

At the change in his countenance, Beth's mouth nearly fell open. Gone was his usual tired, weary expression, replaced with the look of a young, gorgeous man. Tyler Lynch had a headful of wavy brown locks, deep brown eyes that missed nothing and a scar on the right side of his mouth. She'd also noticed he had some scars on his left hand and forearm.

"What are you doing out here instead of inside at the party?" he asked.

The party she'd escaped. "I could ask the same thing of you."

"Which means you're avoiding answering my question?"

Aw, he was sharp, noticing her dodge, but she didn't want to admit even to herself, let alone this man, why she'd escaped the party.

"I thought Charming here needed a heads-up to be extra gentle around Sophie, with her condition and all."

His brow arched. "And what was his answer?"

"He's been bobbing his head, agreeing with me. Besides, he's also making friends with your dog, which surprised both of us."

Dogger looked from her to Tyler as if trying to understand what was happening.

Tyler studied his dog. "Dogger doesn't easily make friends."

She ignored her embarrassment. "I know. I've tried to befriend him before, but he's been very wary around me. What he normally does is give me the eye, turn around and walk off." The words could've applied to Tyler himself. She glanced at him.

Tyler didn't flinch, and Beth breathed a sigh of relief. Instead, he squatted down and ruffled the dog's ears. "Dogger's a survivor and cautious in all he does. Streets of Baghdad do that to a soul."

Looking down at Tyler's brown, wavy hair, Beth had a feeling that Dogger wasn't the only one Tyler was talking about. "Well, I'm glad he's feeling at home enough to invite me to pet him."

Tyler stood and looked at her stocking feet.

"When Dogger sat down in front of Charming, the horse danced a bit, and I wasn't looking and lost my shoes." She ended her explanation in a whisper.

He leaned in to hear the last. Her eyes locked with his and her stomach did a jig. Tyler Lynch was one of the few men she'd known who could see eye to eye with her oldest brother, Ethan, who stood six-foot-three.

Dogger stood and walked closer to Charming, breaking the intimate moment between them. Dogger didn't move while Charming inspected him. Beth knew the two animals were taking stock of each other, much like the man standing next to her. Charming lifted his head and nodded. The dog had passed the test.

Beth stroked Charming's side. "Dogger's on a roll today. Two friends."

The dog glanced over his shoulder as if to say, c'mon, human owner, join me.

Tyler didn't move. Dogger sent him another look.

Beth laughed. "I don't think he's going to give up until you do."

"Okay, okay," Tyler said, holding up his hands. He walked to Charming and rubbed the horse's nose. "I feel kinda funny having the dog introduce us."

Grinning at Tyler's surrender, Beth added, "Sometimes animals have better sense than humans."

Tyler's brow shot up.

She didn't mean it as an insult and wanted to apologize, but decided the best way to correct the situation was to plow on. "How long have you had Dogger?"

His face closed down and his gaze dropped to his hand on Charming's neck. He stroked the gelding's black coat.

Had she gone too far? The man had been as stand-offish as his dog until today and now he was opening up.

"I'm sorry. I didn't mean—"

"I found Dogger under the fender of a car used in a roadside bomb outside of Mosul. I think the poor pup was in the wrong place at the wrong time. We don't know if he was hit by the fender or was in the street and crawled under the fender after it landed close to him.

"I heard the whimper and investigated. There was Dogger, a cute little shaver. He seemed okay except for the cut on the back of his head." He pointed to the scar. "That was where the medic thinks the fender hit him. We adopted him and he became our company's mascot." Tyler glanced down at the dog. "I didn't want to leave him in the country when I came home and none of the other guys at the base wanted to adopt him, so I made arrangements for him to come home with me."

It explained a lot about the two of them. Dogger was never far from Tyler's side.

"Well, I'm glad that he's decided to make friends." Beth leaned down and scratched the dog's head. "I hope he'll want to work with the kids we have coming here, or the other veterans who'll be coming. I think those guys will identify with the dog. He's another survivor."

Tyler continued to stroke Charming. "I'm glad the Army decided to use you all. Anyone say when you'll get your first patient?"

"Next week is when I think we'll get a couple of soldiers. My older brother, Ethan, is training more horses at our parents' ranch to work with adult males."

A spark of interest flared in Tyler's eyes. "Because?"

"Well, you've seen the horses here. Some are taller than others. Brownie is only fourteen hands tall, perfect for the kids who ride. But an adult male will be much too heavy for that little mare. Charming here is right for someone like you."

He jerked. "What?"

"An adult male," she quickly added.

He looked a little less offended.

"You could ride him, but if we have more than one adult male riding at the same time, we'll have to have another horse for them to use."

"Makes sense. It's been a while since I've worked around the barn. When Ollie's here, he's good at directing me."

Oh, goodness, Beth thought, he'd revealed another part of himself. They were on a roll. "Ollie's good at giving orders."

The ranch foreman had been taking chemo for his stomach cancer. Combined with her brother's recent marriage to her college roommate, things had been crazy around the ranch. Beth had also been traveling a great deal as a clothing buyer for the largest independent department store in the state of New Mexico. "I've been praying for him."

Tyler tensed up. It wasn't a big move, just a tightening of his shoulders and expression.

Before she could question him about it, Sophie entered the stables. "Beth, Beth, what are you doing out here?" She looked from Beth to Tyler. "Oh, am I interrupting something?"

Beth flushed to the roots of her hair. Tyler's expression looked like it was carved out of stone.

"Dogger decided to let me pet him. We were just marveling at it."

Sophie took in the scene. "I came out here because I wanted to introduce you to one of the new military riders who's going to start next week."

"I'd love to meet him."

Sophie grinned. "It's a her."

"You're kidding, aren't you?"

"Nope. C'mon and I'll introduce you to Captain Brenda Kaye."

Beth started toward the door but realized she had no shoes on. Sophie looked at her feet.

"You can thank Charming for that," Beth explained. "He kept knocking me into the stall wall and I lost both of my shoes." She hurried back into the stall, found her shoes and slipped them on. Closing the stall door behind her, Beth said, "Okay, I'm ready."

At the stable door, Beth glanced over her shoulder and smiled at Tyler and Dogger.

With her heart light, she walked back to the house with Sophie.

Sophie linked arms with Beth. "What happened back there?"

"He offered his friendship."

Sophie stopped. "Who—the dog or Tyler?"

Beth grinned. "Both."

* * *

Tyler watched Beth and Sophie stroll up the curved walkway to the main house. From their body language, he could tell the women knew each other and were friends. Sophie's dark head leaned close to Beth's light brown curls and they laughed.

Sophie stopped, looked at her friend, then at the stables. Tyler resisted the urge to step back. What had Beth said? They resumed their stroll to the house.

Tyler turned around and walked to Charming's stall where his dog sat. "So, bud, what's going on?"

The dog looked at him, but didn't move from his spot in front of the stall door. The horse stuck his head out and nodded. Tyler didn't know how he felt, but the shock of seeing Dogger allowing Beth to pet him had rocked him back on his heels. Since Tyler had found the wounded pup on that rutted road outside Mosul, there had been a special bond between man and dog. They were both survivors. He'd survived the tornado that killed his parents, and Dogger survived the car explosion. Dogger befriended all the men of his unit, but when the chips were down, Dogger always settled in with Tyler. His best friend and fellow bomb tech, Paul Carter, teased Tyler about what his fiancée was going to think when he showed up in Oklahoma with the mutt who'd want to sleep in the bed between them. They found Dogger a few weeks before Paul died disarming a bomb.

His mind shied away from the painful memory.

Charming whinnied, bringing him back to the present.

Tyler stepped closer and stroked Charming's nose. "Okay, big guy, I get the drift. You want some attention." Tyler had a roll of Lifesavers in his shirt pocket. He grabbed the roll, peeled off one and popped it in his mouth. Charming butted him with his head.

"Want one?"

The horse nodded.

Tyler pulled another candy from the roll and offered it to the horse. He didn't have to offer it twice.

The ghost of a smile curved Tyler's lips.

This afternoon had been chock-full of revelations. Or maybe he should say bombs. When Zach announced at the impromptu party after church that he would become a father, his family and friends had cheered. But Tyler recalled that wounded look that filled Beth's eyes before she quickly looked away. When she turned back, a smile lit her pretty face and she kissed both Sophie and Zach. But there'd been a sadness in her green eyes he'd identified with. He doubted her brother and sister-in-law had noticed it, as focused on their own joy as they were, but he saw it.

Tyler kept careful watch on Beth and saw her slip out of the house and head toward the barn. He tried to talk himself out of it, but followed her, anyway. To do what, he didn't know, but he trusted his instincts. They'd served him well in Iraq.

When he walked into the stables a few minutes ago the shock of what he saw knocked him breathless. Of all the things he expected to see, maybe Beth crying or sitting in a corner having a pity party, her petting Dogger wasn't on his list.

He glanced down at his dog.

"So what's happening, old friend? How come you've decided to become a pal to the folks around here?" For the first time since they'd arrived back from Iraq, Dogger had offered his friendship to a new person. "Not only did you sidle up to Beth, but Charming, too? What's going on?"

Dogger raised his head off his front paws and cocked his head.

It was hard to get used to the idea of Dogger making friends. He felt a slight shift in his feelings about being at the ranch. A little less of an outsider in this family-run business.

After his last tour ended, Tyler didn't re-up, but went home to Oklahoma. It'd been a hard transition, and Dogger had become his lifeline. Tyler didn't have to explain to his dog how he felt, why his moods were all over the map or give details of what happened while he was in theater.

His foster parents wanted to understand, but he felt as if there was a deep chasm between them. And his ex-fiancée didn't want to know anything about his Army days and thought he should shake it off.

Shake it off.

That's why she was his *ex*-fiancée.

Of course, there was his embarrassing reaction at the Fourth of July picnic where some of the youth at the church pulled the prank of setting off cherry bomb firecrackers under the picnic tables where they were seated. He freaked out in front of all the church members, the town council and mayor of their little town. The noise was so similar to the bomb that killed his friend, his instant reaction was to duck. Afterward, when he spotted the boys laughing at everyone, he'd let go with a dressing down that brought the picnic to a halt and tears to the youthful offenders. The gathered witnesses understood Tyler's reaction. No one scolded him, but his fiancée gave him such a look of disgust that Tyler knew the engagement was over, much to his relief.

The next morning Tyler had hugged his foster parents and told them he'd be in contact. His fiancée was nowhere to be seen after the picnic, but she'd left her engagement ring with his foster sister. In the ten months since he'd been gone, he'd called home once, but it didn't go well.

He and Dogger roamed the country until he'd run into Zach McClure in that restaurant in Albuquerque over a month ago. The more he thought about it, the more he knew that "chance" meeting wasn't just chance.

Since being here, something inside him had eased. Of course, that also could be credited to being in the same city as his best buddy's family. He'd finally worked up the nerve to call Paul's mom. She welcomed him with open arms, making him feel even guiltier for not saving Paul's life. Tyler immediately saw the pain in Paul's younger brother eyes and knew this was where he was supposed to be. Somehow, someway, he would try to make up Paul's death to Riley.

Dogger's move today surprised and unsettled Tyler, and yet, oddly enough, he trusted the dog's instincts. Dogger seemed to be able to actually discern a person's heart. Dogger didn't like his ex-fiancée and had growled at her the first time they met. Things had not improved between them. Dogger had pegged her.

"I'm going to need your help with the kid tomorrow. He needs a friend." Tyler squatted by the dog's side and ran his hand over his head. "You'll like him. You liked Paul, and I know you'll like his kid brother."

At least he prayed he would. Tyler would need all the help he could get to win over the reluctant boy.

Tyler sat on the edge of the bed and ran his fingers through his hair. The dream—no nightmare—had seized him again, but before it could end, Dogger woke him.

The dog jumped down from the bed and sat beside Tyler.

"Thanks, boy."

Dogger cocked his head.

Why'd he have *that* dream tonight? He hadn't had the nightmare since he'd started working at Second Chance.

He knew he couldn't go back to sleep, so he slipped on his jeans, grabbed a can of soda from the refrigerator and walked out onto the porch. He parked himself on the top step. At one time, he would've grabbed a beer, but after a bender in Denver that landed him in the hospital, he knew he couldn't drown his problems anymore.

Dogger settled by his side.

"Thanks, bud, for the heads-up." Tyler stroked the dog's head.

The dog had started alerting Tyler when he'd detected the dream and would wake Tyler. The first time Dogger did that they'd just returned stateside, and he was at home with his foster parents. Tyler had started dreaming about Paul's death, but before the dream ramped up, Dogger had jumped on the bed and started licking his face. Tyler woke up with a jerk, coming face-to-face with the dog. It took a moment for his brain to clear and understand what the dog had done. Dogger lay down on the bed and looked at him. His foster parents had run into his room, panicked, and looked helpless. He explained it was just a bad dream. They reluctantly left.

From that time on, Dogger started to sleep beside Tyler. Dogger had been his guard against the nightmare. It also spared him from having his foster parents run into his room and witness him in the throes of the dream.

It had been months since he'd had the dream, so why now?

Popping up the can tab, he took a swallow and thought about what happened this afternoon with Beth. Was that it?

He'd noticed her the first day he'd been here at the ranch. Well, what man with breath wouldn't notice her? With reddish-brown curls that touched her shoulders, intense green eyes and a joyous smile, she attracted people to her like a magnet. She did everything with an enthusiasm that was contagious. He'd seen her talk a grumpy child out of his pout and enjoy the riding lesson.

Her laughter made his heart ache, wanting things that he knew were beyond him now. But as he witnessed Zach's and Sophie's secret smiles and constant touches, it made him yearn for things that could never be. It also made him realize how far off that dream was for him.

Scratching the dog's head, he said, "So you like her, huh? You think the lady needs to be your friend?"

Dogger sat up and cocked his head.

"So what do you see in her that deserves your trust?"

The dog ignored him and settled his head on his paws, leaving Tyler no closer to an answer than he was before.

When he dragged himself to bed an hour later, it was the question he fell asleep thinking about.

Chapter Two

Beth pulled her truck into one of the empty parking spaces behind the stables and grabbed the tote containing her ranch clothes, boots and cowboy hat. She'd been volunteering at the ranch long before Zach started attending therapy sessions for his war injuries. Eventually he fell in love and married the woman running the place, Sophie Powell. Once they bought New Hope Ranch, they renamed it Second Chance Ranch in honor of Zach.

Slipping the tote over her shoulder, she started toward the ranch office needing to change her clothes. She couldn't work with the horses and kids in heels and a straight black skirt. Her quick trip to New York to review the department store's purchases had only taken a few days, and she was glad to make it back for her favorite little girl,

Chelsea, who came weekly for rehabilitation of her legs after the car accident she'd been in.

As Beth walked into the business office, she saw a young kid sitting on a bench by the stable doors. His thin arms were wrapped around his chest and his mouth was compressed into a stubborn line, daring anyone to mess with him.

"Hey, Sophie, how are you feeling today?"

Sophie looked up from her computer screen and took another bite of her banana covered in peanut butter. "Hungry. And the cravings are—let's just say your brother can only shake his head in awe. He tried making a comment when I dipped a sweet pickle into some apricot jam. The fact that I burst out crying made him quickly apologize. Since then, he doesn't comment. Kinda walks quietly around me."

Beth laughed. "It serves him right." She hurried into the bathroom and changed her clothes. Stuffing her heels and skirt into her bag, she walked outside the bathroom, holding her boots and socks. She sat down by Sophie and started to pull on her socks.

"Who's the kid sitting outside the stable door with the don't-talk-to-me look on his face?"

"He's the new kid Tyler wanted to bring to hang around for a while. He's the brother of one of the guys in his unit in Iraq."

"And?"

Sophie shrugged. "Tyler said the kid needs to focus on something else besides his computer games."

"That's it? He didn't offer any other explanation?"

Sophie put down her jar of peanut butter and gave Beth a look. "Tyler has that look on his face that Zach had when he first came here, which told me any other questions I had would be met with a grunt." She shrugged and dipped her finger into the peanut butter. "So I decided not to push it."

Pursuing her lips, Beth shifted them from side to side as she considered the situation. "His reasoning was the kid needs to do more than play computer games? Half the kids in this country fall into that category."

"I know." Sophie licked the peanut butter off her fingers. "There's more to the story, but who was I going to ask? The grumpy kid or the tight-lipped adult?"

A laugh burst out of Beth's mouth. Sophie grinned.

"So that's the lay of the land?"

"Yup, so be careful."

"You make it sound like I'm going to war."

"That's a good way to look at it."

"Thanks, friend. I'll be sure not to take the rejection personally." Beth stepped outside, paused and leaned back through the doorway into the office. "When's Captain Kaye scheduled to start?"

"Tomorrow afternoon. Zach's going to work with her."

"I'll try to be here, too." As Beth strode toward the open stable doors, she noticed the kid hadn't moved, but Dogger had settled at the boy's feet.

Putting on her straw hat, she walked to the stable entrance. The boy tried not to look, but she noticed him peeking at her under his lashes. She stopped by his side and the kid tensed. She didn't have two older brothers and not know how to approach a prickly male.

Beth knelt and held out her hand, and Dogger raised his head and welcomed the touch.

"How you doing?" she asked the dog.

The boy's head came up, surprised that she wasn't talking to him.

"Dogger, I'm jealous," she whispered, leaning toward the dog. "It took you close to a month to offer me your friendship and here you are hanging out with a new person immediately." She sighed. "What am I to think? That you like him more than me?" Continuing to stroke the dog's head, she looked up. "He plays hard to get most of the time."

The boy's eyes widened.

Beth decided not to push her luck, patted Dogger's head, stood and walked into the stables.

She turned around to watch the boy's reaction. He looked over his shoulder, a frown furrowing his brows.

She chuckled and turned around and ran smack-dab into a wide chest. She bounced off it, knocking her hat off. Instantly, the man's hands shot out to steady her. She looked up into Tyler Lynch's deep brown eyes.

"I need to put a bell on you, you know that?" The words popped out of her mouth before she thought.

Tyler's eyes widened, then a deep-throated chuckle rumbled through his chest. The sound filled the dim interior of the stables.

Feeling the electricity to her toes, she smiled back. "I do seem to be in the wrong spot for you, don't I?"

"I'd say so."

He continued to hold her arms, and she wondered if he realized what he was doing. Sadly, his hands fell away and he stepped back.

"Sophie said you brought the young man who is sitting outside. What's his name?"

The humor drained out of his face to be replaced with pain and sadness. "Riley Carter." He rubbed the back of his neck. "His brother was in my unit in Iraq. He was killed disarming a bomb." The words sucked the lightness from the air.

No wonder the kid had an attitude. "I'm so sorry, Tyler."

"Riley took his brother's death real hard. His mother is worried about him and troubled by the chip on his shoulder. Paul told me he was real close to Riley after their father's death. I thought this place might help. I know I've seen some pretty amazing things over the weeks I've been here." He shrugged. "It's worth a shot."

Admiration welled in Beth's heart. His concern for his friend's younger brother spoke well of Tyler. "I think you've got a bit of work ahead of you from the looks of things."

Tyler looked out the open door, again, his expression turning grim. "Yeah, I know."

"Take heart. This ranch is a miraculous place. If it could reach my brother with as bad an attitude as he had when I brought him here, it can work with anyone—" she looked over her shoulder out the open doors "—that young man included."

"You brought Zach here?" Surprise rang in his voice.

Her brows wiggled. "I did. And a pricklier male you've never seen, but he promised me he would try once. I knew Sophie from college and knew she was helping to establish a program for veterans, and I kind of volunteered Zach."

Tyler's brow arched. "How'd he feel about that?"

Beth grinned. "Annoyed. But once he stepped

through the breezeway and saw horses, he was hooked. And he got a wife in the bargain."

"I hope it's that easy with Riley—with the exception of the wife thing."

"Ah, there were a few bumps. You might not realize it, but Riley's bad attitude is encouraging. I think he's fighting a battle within himself. He's curious, but that male pride thingie is standing in his way. We've got to figure out a way he can save face and start exploring things here."

"What do you mean, that 'male pride thingie'?"

Beth laughed at his indignant tone and reached down, picking up her hat. "I rest my case." With those words, she put on her hat and walked to the tack room to get Charming's bridle. She'd let Mr. Macho wrestle with the ideas she just floated. Riley wasn't the only prickly male around the stables.

Beth finished with her last rider of the day, Chelsea. The little girl had the heart of a lion, enduring surgery after surgery to correct the damage done in the car accident. Her legs, broken in multiple places, had healed, but her gait was still awkward. Since she'd started riding, her attitude had changed and her coordination had improved.

Beth helped Chelsea off the horse. The eight-year-old grinned from ear to ear.

"I love Brownie." She patted the horse's side.

"Why don't you go get a carrot for her?" Beth asked.

The little girl hurried to the carrot barrel and grabbed a short one. She fed it to Brownie. Chelsea's mother smiled at her daughter.

"It's a miracle," she said to Beth, her eyes glistening with emotion. "She can run, even if it is slowly."

Beth knew the feeling. "It is." She tied Brownie to the iron ring in the wall by the mounting stairs and walked out with mom and daughter. Turning, she expected to see a pouty Riley, but the bench stood empty. She'd tried several times this afternoon to involve Riley in some small way with the horses and riders. She suggested giving a carrot to one of the horses or getting bridles from the tack room, but the kid steadfastly refused to be interested in anything. She'd gotten only grunts and one-word answers.

Looking around the ring, Beth tried to spot Riley, thinking he might have broken down and gotten interested in something. He'd been a fixture on the bend for the past three hours, glaring at all the people who came close to him. She fought down the panic and rushed down the breezeway on the far side of the office that led to the parking lot. Scanning the cars, she saw no sign of the boy. Turning back to the yard, she realized she didn't see Dogger, either.

Running back to the office, she opened the door. "Sophie, have you seen the kid that Tyler brought?"

Sophie stood and glanced out the office window. "No. Why?"

"Because he's not over there, and I can't find him anywhere."

Sophie hurried out from behind the desk. "Okay, I'll get Ollie and Zach and see if we can find him."

"Great, I'll check with Tyler. Maybe he took the kid home."

The women headed in different directions. Sophie walked out into the ring where Zach worked with a rider, while Beth headed back into the stables. She found Tyler behind the stables moving sacks of feed into the storage room.

"I can't find Riley. Is he with you?"

He stopped. "No."

"He's not sitting on the bench, and I've looked around and can't find him. Dogger's also missing."

Tyler took off his leather gloves. "Are you sure?"

"Yes. I tried to get Riley to help this afternoon with some of the clients, but he refused. He was there when I started working with my last rider."

Tyler shoved his gloves into his back pocket.

The pulse in his neck throbbed, but his voice didn't reflect any panic. "I'll check the corral behind the stables. Have you looked through each stall in the stable?"

"No. I'll check them." She raced back to the stables, praying they'd find the boy.

Tyler fought back the alarm gripping his heart. Fear never led to good results, as the Army had taught him. He needed a clear head. His military training came flooding back. He surveyed the corral behind the stables sprawling out before him. He found himself whispering a prayer under his breath. He figured that God wouldn't be offended if he prayed for the boy.

There were two horses out in the corral, but no sign of Riley or Dogger. Thinking of his dog, some of his alarm eased. Dogger would take care of the kid. The dog's instincts had saved Tyler in the field more than once.

He walked down the path to the river beyond the riding corrals, making his way along the path. There was no sign of the boy.

He spotted Zach and Sophie through the trees. "You see anything?"

"Nothing," Zach called back. "You know how long he's been missing?"

"I saw him sitting on that bench less than twenty minutes ago."

"He can't have gone far." Zach stepped on a rock and his artificial leg folded under him. He caught himself on a tree branch.

Sophie's face lost all color. "Are you okay?" she asked, putting her arm around his back.

Zach nodded.

Tyler appeared by Zach's side. He didn't offer his help, but was there if Zach needed anything. Zach pushed away from the tree and met Tyler's gaze. Zach nodded his thanks.

"I think my dog's with Riley," Tyler said getting back to the subject. "He'll take care of the kid."

"How did this happen?" Sophie asked. "How could he have disappeared so quickly? I looked out the office window not ten minutes ago, and he was there, his frown firmly in place."

Sophie glanced at Tyler, her embarrassment clear in her blush. "Ugh—sorry."

"Don't worry about it," Tyler reassured her. "It's the truth. I'd hoped…" There was no point in explaining.

They turned and walked back to the stables. Tyler heard Beth's voice floating outside through the open doors.

"There you are, Dogger. Have you taken up with your new friend?"

Tyler hurried into the dark interior of the building, dread riding him hard. He understood Riley's heart, understood the fear and resentment the boy held on to as if it were a talisman. Riley hadn't verbally said how he felt, but Tyler recognized the emotions coloring the boy's eyes. And Tyler knew if Beth rained all over the kid, he'd retreat further into himself, where no one would be able to reach him.

Tyler strode down the center aisle like an avenging angel, ready to do battle to protect the boy. He scanned the area for Beth and Riley. He heard Beth, but didn't see her.

"I missed you guarding that doorway," she continued. "Then you went off, wandering around with Tyler's friend."

Her voice came from the second to last stall before the open double doors, leading to the back corral. He made it close enough to see the floor of the stall. Beth sat beside Dogger. Riley sat on the other side of the dog.

He opened his mouth, but Beth beat him. "You've got to be a great guy," she told Riley as she scratched the dog's head.

Riley glanced at her, his mouth hanging open.

"I told you Dogger's mighty selective about his friends, and if he's hanging with you, I'd say you have his seal of approval. Can you tell me your secret?"

The youth's eyes widened.

"You see, I've got other kids coming here to ride, and I'm hoping that Dogger can help them as much as the horses do. You seem to have charmed him, so what's your secret?"

Her question surprised Tyler as much as it did Riley. What happened next surprised Tyler even more. The boy smiled shyly and glanced at her. He shrugged his thin shoulders. "Don't know."

Beth scratched Dogger's side and he rolled onto his back to give her better access to his belly. The dog did that with Tyler or Paul, but with the other guys in Tyler's unit the dog never showed them that level of trust.

He heard another person enter the stables. Glancing over his shoulder, he spotted Zach. When Zach opened his mouth, Tyler shook his head.

"C'mon," Beth urged. "Think about it. You've got a talent, so maybe you can share it with others."

Riley reached out and rubbed Dogger's stomach. One rub, then he snatched his hand back. "I let Dogger come to me."

Beth nodded her head. "That makes sense. Come to think of it, I did that, too. I didn't try to pet him at first, but let him think about it, and when he was ready, he approached me." Beth's smile brought light to this corner of the stables. "So, I'll warn the kids to let Dogger approach them." She rested her back against the wall. "Thank you for that insight."

Another miracle occurred. Riley's chest puffed out and he reached out again and rubbed Dogger's stomach.

"How she does that I don't know," Zach whispered.

Tyler glanced at his friend. Zach motioned for Tyler to join him outside. The two men walked out into the sunlight.

"Does your sister do that often?" Tyler asked, impressed by how Beth had handled the exchange between Riley and herself.

Shaking his head, Zach laughed. "When we were growing up, she had a talent to read Ethan and me, then rat us out to my folks. Of course, when it came to the guys she dated, she was useless, but that may be the brother in me talking."

Before Tyler could comment, Susan Carter rounded the corner of the office. "How's it going?"

Tyler didn't have the heart to explain about losing her son for a brief time. "I think we've made a little progress. My dog's attached himself to Riley. And Riley smiled."

"Really," she whispered, relief lighting her face. Her gaze went from Tyler to Zach. He nodded the truth of Tyler's statement. "Oh, I've prayed and prayed."

Tyler swallowed. "Come with me and I'll show you."

* * *

"Are you upset?" Beth asked as she stopped by Tyler's side. He was brushing down Charming. Susan and Riley had left close to a half hour ago.

His hand stilled on the horse's flank. "What are you talking about?"

"Are you upset about me talking to Riley?" She craned her neck so she could see his eyes. Her head almost rested on Charming's side. Tyler met her gaze.

"No."

Oh, that male mind-set, say as little as you can to get yourself out of trouble. "Would you care to expand on that?"

He went back to brushing the horse.

She didn't move, blocking his access to the horse's front shoulder. She had two brothers and knew how to outwait a stubborn male, and she wanted an answer.

"What do you want me to say?"

Progress. "I saw that panicked look on your face when I was sitting with Riley. You looked like I was fixin' to put my foot in it and scare the poor kid."

He flushed. "You saw that?"

"I did."

Shrugging, he gave Charming a final stroke, then put the brush on the shelf. "I knew from experience that the more you push with a boy that age, the further you push them away."

Beth heard the pain in his voice, startling her. What had happened to this man that he could identify with Riley's situation? "You've been there and done that."

He remained silent for so long that she feared she'd pushed him too hard. "I'm s—"

"Yeah."

She knew this time to give the man room, but he surprised her.

"When I went into foster care, the social worker wanted me to spill my guts." He untied Charming from the ring on the wall and led him back to his stall.

Beth stared after his retreating form. He starts to spill his guts and then walks away?

She hurried after him. "You can't leave me hanging there. What happened?"

"Why do you care?"

If he'd slapped her, she couldn't have been more startled. Instinctively, she stepped back. Scrambling to come up with an answer, she said, "I want to understand how to help Riley. You have an insight that will help me to help him."

Tyler put Charming in his stall, then slipped the halter off of the horse's head. He paused, studying her. "Makes sense. I ran through five foster care homes in two years. I think I held the record for that part of Oklahoma. I was known as a trouble-maker until I got to the Olaskys." His gaze turned inward. "They didn't ask me to open up. They gave me the room I needed and respected me." He gave a soft laugh. "But I got toted to church and that's where the Lord got ahold of me. After that, I was willing to talk."

Working hard not to show her surprise, Beth said, "You had some wise foster parents."

He paused. "I did."

"When was the last time you saw them? Are they still alive?"

His expression closed down. "They are still alive."

It didn't take a genius to realize she'd touched a raw nerve. The glacial change in him happened so fast it took her breath away. Redirect him.

"Well, I hope we made a breakthrough with Riley. Of course, it's my experience that boys his age can change in an instant. Oh, I remember one time when I asked Ethan if I could borrow his western bolo tie to wear to the rodeo. He said yes. We watched him at the steer-wrestling competition that afternoon." She remembered how the little calf had dragged her brother around the arena. "He was the only one who didn't wrestle down his cow and he ate a lot of dirt. Well, after the rodeo, the first person he saw was me, wearing his tie. He pitched a fit and demanded his tie back there at the arena. So let's pray that Riley will be feeling cheerful the next time we see him."

Tyler tried not to smile, but her story broke the ice. "We'll see."

She took a deep breath, knowing she'd averted disaster. "I'll check the horses on the other side of the row and make sure they have fresh hay." Not waiting for his reply, she walked down the aisle.

Tyler had revealed another layer of himself and her heart whispered he was a good man. He'd slipped past the shield she'd erected around her heart. And oddly enough, that realization didn't panic her.

Tyler snapped his fingers, calling for Dogger. The dog raced out of the stall and joined him at the door.

"What's come over you, friend? Suddenly you're Mr. Social, rolling over and letting anyone scratch your belly."

"Are you expecting him to answer you?" Zach asked, walking up to the stables.

"I've gotta stop talking out loud."

"Yeah, my sister can drive any male to talk to himself."

Tyler threw a grin at his friend. "What I don't understand is why Dogger's decided to make friends with your sister and Riley. It's put me off my stride, so why shouldn't I expect him to answer me?" Tyler had discussed with Zach what he wanted to do with Riley. They both agreed that horses would benefit the boy.

Zach stepped to the fence enclosing the ring in front of the stables. He rested his forearms on the top rail. "This place changed me, so maybe Dogger's following suit."

Tyler joined him. "So I heard."

With a laugh, Zach said, "That's the trouble with sisters. They volunteer your secrets along with advice on how to fix things."

Tyler tried to keep a straight face, but didn't manage it. "That's true."

"When I came here, the first time I rode I tired myself out. Too much pride to tell anyone about my weakness, so when I got off Charming, I fell and my brother caught me. Afterward, Beth asked, 'How do you feel?'" He shook his head. "I wanted to snarl 'how do you think?' but then I looked at that sincere face and knew I couldn't dump on her." He grinned and glanced at Tyler. "Of course, it *was* the stupidest question she'd ever asked."

Tyler understood exactly how Zach felt. "I've got my share of stupid, too."

Zach didn't say anything for several minutes, but they looked out over the corrals and down the hill toward the setting sun. There was a stillness and a peacefulness here that called to Tyler's soul.

"Beth might be pushy, but you know if it hadn't been for her, I'd still be stewing in my pity. Of course, she doesn't know when to mind her own business and back off. She means well and her heart is in the right place." Zach pushed away from the fence. "You'll just have to take her actions as trying to help. She's dealt with me. Brace yourself, because it's going to happen again. Ignore it."

"Will ignoring her help?"

Zach's mouth twitched. "No. And my brother Ethan can second me."

"Thanks for the warning."

As Zach walked away, Tyler didn't know how he felt. So Beth wasn't going to quit. It didn't make sense, but Tyler was grateful Beth McClure wasn't going to give up her fight.

Yeah, he was glad that little dynamo wouldn't quit. Not only for Riley's sake, but his. The thought unsettled him.

Walking up to the foreman's house, Riley knew deep in his spirit that God had put her in his life.

He didn't know how he felt about that, but he found himself smiling.

Tyler looked down at Dogger. "So what do you think? You like her, too?"

Dogger ran up the stairs and faced his master, his tongue out.

"You're not going to answer until I feed you. Okay, chow, then I expect an answer."

"I'm glad you stayed for dinner," Sophie told Beth.

Both Zach and Beth cleared the dishes. Sophie put the leftover lasagna in a plastic container.

"Well, you twisted my arm until I yelled uncle." Beth popped one of the cherry tomatoes in her mouth as she carried the remains of the salad to the kitchen.

Stepping to her side, Zach pulled a strand of her hair just as he had so often in the past when they were growing up. She could only thank God for restoring her brother after he lost his leg.

"What were you going to have, sis? A burger purchased in a drive-thru or a frozen dinner?" He wagged his brows.

She could act outraged or admit Zach had nailed it on the head. "If you must know, it was going to be a burger."

Zach hugged her and glanced at Sophie. "Do I know my sister or what?"

Sophie shooed him away with her hands. "Go, before I let your sister smack you with one of the skillets."

Grinning unrepentantly, he escaped into the living room and turned on the news.

Beth and Sophie worked together to clean up the kitchen.

"This reminds me of college," Sophie said as she filled the sink with soapy water. She rubbed the small of her back.

"Go and sit. Or exchange places with my brother. You need to get off your feet."

When Sophie didn't argue, Beth knew she'd read her friend correctly. Sophie settled at the table and put her feet on a chair. "You remember that party we went to our sophomore year at Janelle's apartment? And remember she got so sick on the chicken?"

The memory of that disastrous party flashed before Beth's eyes. Janelle had brought some chicken from a local hole-in-the wall café and the stuff had given everyone food poisoning. Beth and Sophie were the only two who stayed with the pizza and the only ones not moaning and throwing up. "That was bad."

"And you remember your date got it, too."

"Yeah, he turned green, heaved and left the apartment without any explanation."

"Well, consider yourself lucky, 'cause my date, who was his roommate, if you remember, heaved on my shoes while telling me they were going home." Once their dates split, Beth and Sophie were stuck at the apartment without a car. "We lucked out that Janelle lived close to the bus line that ran by our dorm."

Sophie studied her and frowned. "You know." Sophie cocked her head as if a revelation occurred to her. "There were always guys around you, but we all went together as a group. I can't think of—"

Beth looked up from the sink. "Of what?"

Sophie's eyes narrowed. "Of any man you dated more than once while we were in college."

Putting the last dish in the drainer, Beth dried her hands. She settled across the table from Sophie. "I never found anyone who could live up to my standards. I have a wonderful, generous father who is perfect."

"True. But you have a couple of brothers with flaws."

"I won't argue there."

"But you never—"

The direction of this conversation made Beth uncomfortable. Back then, the lack of a boyfriend had been intentional. "You know, your pregnancy is making you want to mother everyone."

Sophie leaned across the table and took Beth's hand. "Be careful, friend. Remember, lots of our soldiers return to civilian life with baggage, and Tyler has his share."

Beth jerked her hand away. "I know that. Remember who hauled Zach here."

"True, but I see something in your eyes, Beth. Please be careful."

Sophie's comment cut too close to the truth. "Sophie, I understand the man has issues. I'm not sure he can carry on a conversation. I've only heard one-word answers or grunts." Beth's mind flashed to the conversations she'd had with Tyler. Those were exceptions, she told herself.

Sophie laughed, making Beth chuckle.

"You've got that nailed, but there's something—" Sophie shook her head.

Beth opened her mouth to protest, but Sophie held up her hand.

"I'm just warning you."

Beth couldn't hold her friend's words against her. She came around the table and kissed Sophie's cheek. "Thank you."

"You'll pay attention to my warning?"

"I will."

Later that night as Beth drifted off to sleep, she tried to tell herself that because Sophie was pregnant she was seeing things.

Deep inside, Beth knew Sophie had been right.

Chapter Three

It had been the longest ten days of Beth's life. She used to love to travel for work, seeing different cities, flying off at the drop of a hat, but this last trip to London, then to Dallas, had been more than tedious. Her heart had stayed at Second Chance Ranch with a silent man, his dog and a troubled boy. In the quiet of morning when she had her coffee and read her Bible, she found herself praying for Tyler and Riley and longing to see how things were progressing with them.

It occurred to Beth that this was the first time since her disastrous relationship with her high school boyfriend ended that she found herself overwhelmed by attraction. She tried to chalk her feelings up to compassion for a hurt child and an emotionally wounded soldier. Would she be that intense with each new military rider? She ignored the uncomfortable question.

What had happened in Tyler's life that caused him to be put into foster care? That question rumbled around her brain the entire time she was on her business trip and she planned to see if Zach knew about Tyler's past.

Parking in the ranch's lot, she planned her strategy—corner Zach and put the screws on. When she reached the ranch office, she found no one there. After changing, Beth walked to the stables. Two riders were out in the two rings. Sophie supervised one rider and Tyler was in the second ring, walking beside a new boy who looked terrified. Observing from his regular perch by the door sat Riley.

Beth stopped by Riley's side. "How's it going?"

The boy shrugged.

Hadn't they got past this? "Where's Dogger?"

Another shrug.

"Do you know the boy Tyler's helping?"

"No."

What had happened to put Riley back to square one? She walked into the stables, hoping to find Zach. Two other volunteers were inside working on different horses. She waved to them, and then spotted Ollie coming out of the tack room. He'd just about finished his chemo, and he was looking good and starting to gain back some weight.

"Ollie, have you seen Zach?"

"He's out back with Ethan, checking out the new horse the ranch got."

"That's good news. Where did we get it?"

"Ask your brother."

"Which one, Zach or Ethan?"

"Zach."

What she needed to do was to talk to Sophie to know what was really going on at the ranch instead of wasting time trying to get info from Zach. "You're looking good."

"I'll say I don't feel like dirt no more, so that's an improvement."

"Quit charming me with your words."

"Get out of here." Affection laced his words.

Stepping out the side doors of the stables, she saw Zach on a new horse, riding the gelding around the corral. The bay had a black mane and tail and black stockings on all four feet. Ethan stood at the fence, watching.

"Where'd you get that handsome horse?" Beth called out.

Ethan turned and smiled at Beth. "Hey, girl. Good to see you home." He opened his arms, and she walked into them.

"I'm glad to be home. What are you doing here? Is this your day to volunteer?"

He shook his head. "Zach called and wanted me to see our newest mount. To evaluate him."

"So, where'd the horse come from?"

Ethan turned back to watch Zach. "You want to tell her, Zach, since the guy talked to you?"

Zach brought the horse up to the gate. "A rancher in the west of the state read about our new program for veterans, and since he's a Vietnam vet, he wanted to help. He thought Dusty here would be perfect. He dropped him off yesterday."

"He's a good-looking horse. Perfect for the soldiers."

Zach dismounted easily. If you didn't know the man, you would never guess his right leg was artificial. "You're right."

Beth watched him for a minute, then asked, "What's with Riley?"

Zach threw his brother a look, opened the corral gate and walked the horse out.

She knew Zach had ignored her question about Riley. "Why's Riley sitting outside on the bench pouting again? Did something happen?"

Rubbing the horse's nose, Zach glanced at her. "Nothing that I know about."

"That doesn't make sense."

"Sis, he's a thirteen-year-old boy," Ethan answered. "He doesn't need a reason to glare and have a bad attitude. You should know, having grown up with brothers."

Beth looked from one brother to the other. "True enough, but I thought we got over that hump."

Ethan grinned. "I think that's my cue to leave. I wanted to tell you all that the doctor got a bad kick from one of the horses he was examining on our last horse rescue. He's limping badly. Pray for him."

Doctor Adams had been the vet for her parents' ranch for the past twenty years. He was the only vet for the ranches around that part of the state. He also came out to Second Chance to care for the horses. "I'm sorry to hear that. Has Doc thought about getting a new associate? I mean Doc doesn't move as fast as he did twenty years ago and can't dodge the kicks from the stock as quickly as he once could."

The brothers exchanged an unvoiced message.

"It's the truth," Beth defended herself.

Ethan kissed her cheek. "I'm out of here." He walked toward his truck.

Beth knew a strategic retreat when she saw one.

Zach didn't comment, but walked the new horse into the stables. Sophie trailed him inside and helped unsaddle the horse.

"You said his name was Dusty." She nodded toward the horse.

"That's right." Zach pulled the saddle off the gelding's broad back. Beth got the saddle blanket and put it on the stand beside the saddle.

"What do you want?"

Beth wanted to grind her teeth. Her strategy wasn't working. "What makes you think I want something?"

Her brother stared at her over the horse's back. "The last time you helped me unsaddle a horse, you were eleven and wanted to pump me for information about what Mom and Dad knew about your adventure in the barn when you dropped the paint from the loft."

Sometimes it didn't pay to have a smart brother. "What do you know about Tyler's background?"

"Why do you want to know?" He grabbed a curry brush and started to work on the horse's back.

"He mentioned going from foster home to foster home." She picked up the other brush and started on Dusty's other side.

"Butt out, Sis. Tyler doesn't need you to understand him. He's doing a great job, and he'll handle Riley."

Zach had that look that told her she wasn't going to get any more answers out of him. "Okay." She put the brush back on the shelf and started to walk out of the grooming area.

Zach's hand shot out, stopping her. "That's it? You're giving up?"

She rubbed Dusty's forehead and smiled at her brother. "What do you think?"

He shook his head and turned back to the horse. "You're not going to listen to me."

"Remember who dragged you here."

"That's what I was afraid of," he mumbled as he continued brushing the horse.

After Beth finished working with her first rider, she knew she couldn't let Riley pout the rest of the afternoon. It went against her grain. She remembered what her mother said to her father the day after her brothers had a major fight. She didn't worry about their attitude. Just keep them busy, and the attitude would fix itself. Well, if it worked with her two stubborn brothers, it couldn't hurt trying it with Riley. Of course, her brother would accuse her of meddling, but her heart wouldn't allow her to ignore a child in pain, no matter how her brothers would interpret it.

Walking to the bench, she said, "Hey, Riley, I need some help."

"Huh?"

Boys were so articulate. "C'mon, I need you to help me."

He straightened. Dogger, who rested at his feet, sat on his haunches. "I don't know nothin' about horses."

"We can change that."

He looked around, seeing if anyone was watching.

"Just imagine all the things you can tell the kids at school. You can impress them. Brag and be the expert. And girls adore horses and the men who know about them."

She watched him think about it, then he nodded, stood and walked into the stables.

"Okay, let's get Brownie's tack."

"What?"

"Her bridle, reins and saddle blanket. We're going to get her ready for the next rider."

Beth explained to the boy what was needed and showed him where the little horse's equipment was stored. She took her time to explain everything to him. Riley, in spite of himself, showed interest. When he found himself being eager, he fixed the scowl on his face.

He put the bridle on the horse, then settled the blanket on the horse's back.

"Okay, since our rider, Chelsea is her name, is going to be riding Brownie, let's attach each stirrup to the blanket. Remember, she's not a tall girl."

The boy buckled the stirrup to the blanket.

"Hey, what's going on here?" Tyler stood behind Riley.

Beth stabbed Tyler with her gaze. "We're getting Brownie ready for her rider. I asked Riley for his help. He's done a great job."

Riley tried to appear bored, but his eyes twinkled.

Beth didn't let Tyler's questioning look stop her,

and pulled Brownie's lead reins. "C'mon, Riley, let me show you how we use side walkers to help the riders who need it."

"I don't know—"

She waved off the rest of the comment. "I know a little girl who'd like a young man like you to help her."

Riley glanced over his shoulder. Tyler shrugged. Turning back to Beth, he said, "I guess I can try."

Swallowing the grin that fought to erupt, Beth led Riley and Brownie to the mounting steps, but she could feel Tyler's gaze burning into her back.

Tyler watched as Riley followed Beth like a puppy. He couldn't quite believe how she charmed the kid again. The other day she got a smile out of him and now she had him out helping with one of the riders. The woman had a touch, and not only with Riley. He felt himself opening up to her, looking forward to seeing her again.

Following them to the mounting steps, he watched Beth instruct Riley. There was another adult standing ready by the steps, but she showed Riley how to help guide the girl's shoe into the stirrup. It was too short, so Beth had Riley read-just the stirrup. The boy's chest puffed out.

How'd the woman do it? She'd certainly captivated Dogger. Since that day, he found himself thinking about her. What was it about the woman that drew hi—Dogger. His dog didn't offer his friendship to just anyone. He recalled the guys in his unit. Dogger accepted them all and allowed them to pet him, but the guys who were a little out of control, the dog stayed away from. And, of course, Dogger loved Paul. Dogger grieved for Paul, too.

Not only had Tyler been thinking about Beth, but he had been thinking of God, too, and his relationship with Him. Tyler had seen the Bible in the bookcase and pulled it out. He hadn't opened it, but he'd left it on the coffee table.

Watching Riley now, Tyler saw reflections of Paul. Riley's expression of concentration mirrored Paul's. How often had they disarmed bombs or worked an explosion, trying to analyze how the bomb, car or pipe, was constructed.

He closed his eyes, wanting to shut out the pain. If Paul had only waited a few more seconds for him to get the right pliers...but he was sure he knew how to disarm it. In the end, it wouldn't have mattered, since the timer was a decoy. The bomber had been in the restaurant and waited until he knew the Americans were there before he hit the remote trigger, detonating it.

The sorrow and regret slammed into Tyler, robbing him of breath. Turning, he walked through the stables and out the side door. Maybe he could outrun the pain. He'd tried to drink away the memories, but they never went away. After his last round with the drink where he landed in the hospital, the VA doctors told him if he didn't stop, he wouldn't have a liver. They recommended counseling to deal with the survivor's guilt.

That afternoon he wandered into the VFW post in Denver. One of the older guys fed him and gave him milk to drink. He hadn't had milk in years, but it reminded Tyler of his mom and dad and the farm they owned before the tornado destroyed it, killing both of them.

What would his mother think of her son if she saw him a homeless drunk? Or his grandmother who took him in after his parents' death?

Then the veteran did the most amazing thing. He prayed with Tyler. He didn't know how he felt about that. He'd been saved when he was in his teens, but after Paul's death, he couldn't pray. How could a merciful God allow his entire family to die, one by one, and then his best friend? The last thing the old guy said was, until Tyler settled his anger with God, nothing would be right, and he invited him to chapel that night. Tyler wasn't ready to hear from God and didn't go. That day, he quit drinking, but his spirit remained unsettled.

A bark broke into Tyler's thoughts. Glancing down, he found Dogger at his feet.

"What?"

The dog settled his chin on Tyler's foot. Tyler

squatted and ran his hand over the dog's head. "Are you telling me to snap out of it?"

The dog's eyes met his master's.

"Okay. I need to think about what I can do to help Riley." He scratched the dog's head. "But it still hurts, friend."

"What hurts?"

Tyler looked up at Sophie.

"Did you strain something? Or are you feeling sick?"

Tamping down his embarrassment, Tyler slowly stood. "No, I'm not sick, but you did catch me talking to my dog, which could make you wonder about my sanity."

She waved the comment away. "Then I'd have to wonder about Zach and myself. I spent more time talking to Charming than anyone when Zach started coming here. Charming helped me a lot of nights."

Tyler breathed a sigh of relief. Sophie didn't think he needed a shrink.

"The reason I'm here is Riley's mom is on the phone."

"Is anything wrong?"

"I don't know. She didn't seem too panicked."

Tyler's heart slowed down and followed Sophie to the phone by the entrance to the stables.

"She's on line two."

He picked up the hand set and pushed line two. "Tyler here."

"I'm so glad I got you, Tyler. I have a favor to ask. My business meeting is running late, and I'm not going to make it over there before about eight. Could Riley stay with you until I'm finished?"

He didn't know how he felt, but he couldn't refuse. "Sure."

"Thank you. This meeting got delayed and there's no way I can leave."

"It's okay, Susan. We'll get something to eat."

"Oh, you don't have to do that."

He laughed. "Susan, he's a thirteen-year-old boy. Yes, I do."

"You've got a point. He's eating everything in the kitchen, even fruit."

"Don't worry. I've got it covered."

"Thank you, Tyler." Her voiced vibrated with emotions.

"I'm happy to do it."

"I'll give you a call when I'm on the way to pick Riley up."

"You're covered." He hung up. Well, it didn't matter if he or Riley were prepared to do this. They were about to bond.

When he knew he wasn't being watched, excitement shone in Riley's eyes. Beth wanted to laugh with delight, but knew the move would shut the boy down.

But the excitement she felt nearly overwhelmed her. Riley stood taller as he walked beside the rider. He tried to act cool, but his excitement and pride bubbled up.

Chelsea carefully made her way down the steps. Once on the ground, she smiled. "Did you see that?" she crowed. "I did it myself."

Riley's shoulders went back.

"I did see that," Beth replied. "What an improvement."

She walked into her mother's arms. "I did it, Momma."

Mother and daughter hugged, thanked them and left.

"Okay, Riley, let me show you how to care for Brownie now. You're Brownie's caretaker and need to be responsible to unsaddle her, rub her down and make sure she has feed."

He nodded and followed Beth.

They were settling Brownie in her stall when Tyler found them.

"How'd the afternoon go?"

Riley shrugged.

"He was great." Beth volunteered the praise. The boy deserved it. "I think he's going to be a natural."

Riley rolled his eyes, but Beth could tell the

words pleased him when the corner of his mouth curved up.

Tyler glanced at her and they shared a moment of pride. "Riley, I just got a call from your mother. She has a meeting that is running late and told me it might be eight before she gets here."

"What?" Riley's eyes grew large and he glanced around. "I've got to get home and—" His stomach growled and a red stain crept up his neck. "And I'm hungry. What does she think I'm going to do for food?"

Signs of his panic screamed at Beth and she wanted to head off disaster. "I'm hungry, too."

Riley's mouth hung open and he stared at her.

"How about you, Tyler? You hungry, too?" Beth prayed he understood her effort to divert the boy.

"I am."

Stepping toward Riley, she asked, "How about we go to the burger place down the road? That little place has the best burgers within fifty miles. When I want to treat myself, I go there."

Riley looked from Beth to Tyler. The alarm drained out of his expression. "Yeah, okay, that sounds good."

She slipped her arm around Riley's skinny shoulders. "Thank you for agreeing to go. I can't tell you how much I needed an excuse to stop there." Grinning, she whispered, "None of the trendy people go there. It's got big, greasy burgers in giant buns and the fries are to die for—" she closed her eyes and moved her head from side to side "—and my friends are all health nuts, wanting me to eat alfalfa sprouts and wheatgrass and all the things my cows eat. I can simply tell them I'm helping feed a young man who worked hard."

Riley's chin came up. "Sure."

Beth smiled at Tyler. The man simply shook his head.

"Then let's finish with this horse, get the truck and go get burgers."

"Okay." Riley went to put up Brownie's bridle. Tyler stood staring at the boy.

"You're welcome," Beth whispered in his ear.

He jerked back. "What?"

"I was simply responding to your thank-you."

"But I didn't say anything," he protested.

She gave him a look that said "I know" and walked off, chuckling to herself.

Chapter Four

Tyler watched in awe as Riley inhaled the last onion ring. The boy hadn't been shy about downing the burger and large fries he'd ordered. Beth had offered Riley some of her onion rings and he'd eagerly accepted them and devoured the remaining ones.

Tyler tried to hold back his smile, but when his eyes met Beth's and saw the amusement dancing there, his smile emerged.

Riley sat back and sighed.

"Are you full?" Beth asked.

"It was good, and I won't rat you out to your friends."

Beth's mouth trembled as she tried to suppress her giggle. "I appreciate that."

Riley, sensing the light mood, grinned. "I know my mom sometimes gets on a kick to make me eat healthylike. She wants me to eat lettuce, tomatoes and other green junk."

"Junk?" Beth asked, looking at Tyler, then Riley.

"Yeah, that other green stuff—broccoli, cabbage and other things like that."

Beth nodded, trying to be stern, but the humor in the air took the sting out of her comment. "Your mom's right. Vegetables are important, but an occasional burger—"

"With fries."

"—is okay. But the vegetables are important."

He shrugged. "Whatever."

Tyler chuckled, welcoming the joy and mirth of the evening. He couldn't remember the last time he'd laughed.

"If we're going to splurge, those fried pies look good." Riley nodded toward the display of desserts on the order counter. He looked from Tyler to Beth with a hangdog expression. The boy knew how to work a crowd.

Tyler shrugged and pulled out a couple of dollars from his wallet. Riley grinned, took the money and raced to the counter before anyone could object.

Leaning across the table, Beth whispered, "I hope his mother isn't going to be mad at us."

"Don't worry. Susan will be grateful when she sees her son grinning and eating and trying to get his way."

Riley appeared at the table with the fried pie. "Cherry." He quickly unwrapped the treat and took a bite. "'tis good," he mumbled around the crust and cherries.

"I have a weakness for the coconut," Beth admitted. "They make their own pies."

Riley nodded and downed the rest of the pie in a few bites, followed by gulps of his soft drink. "I could use another one of those."

"I think you'll get Tyler in trouble with your mom if you're on too much of a sugar high. She might not want to trust Tyler again."

Riley studied Tyler, considering, then nodded. "Okay."

Tyler's gut eased. He wanted to establish a relationship with Riley, but Tyler didn't want to alienate Riley's mom, either.

"But, you might win some points if you brought a fried pie to your mom," Beth added.

The boy's shoulders straightened. "I like that idea, but I don't have enough money."

"Not a problem. I'm going to get a pie for myself and save it for my breakfast tomorrow," she whispered in a conspiratorial tone.

With the speed that only a thirteen-year-old boy could have, Riley jumped up and ran to the window. Tyler pulled another bill from his wallet. When Beth opened her mouth to object, he nodded his head. "My treat."

Her gaze locked with his, and he felt her response down to his toes.

"Thanks."

"Not a problem."

Beth slipped out of her chair and joined Riley at the order counter.

Tyler watched Beth, rattled by their unspoken exchange. It was only a fried pie, he told himself. But for Tyler, he knew he'd crossed some invisible line. He couldn't identify it, but something in his heart had changed.

"How did you start at the ranch?" Riley asked as they drove back from the burger joint. Riley sat between Beth and Tyler in the front seat of the truck.

"I grew up on a ranch." She turned toward Riley. "I've been around horses all my life. When I was in grade school, I did barrel racing."

"Really?" Riley's face filled with amazement.

"I had a beautiful little horse that loved to race. She was the one who kept me practicing. When I didn't want to race, Milly, my horse, would remind me I hadn't worked with her that day. Can you imagine being nagged by your horse?"

Riley's jaw hung open. "You're fooling me."

"Nope. Sometimes, Milly was worse than a big puppy, wanting my attention."

"I don't believe that."

Beth glanced over at Tyler. From his expression, she knew he was enjoying this exchange.

"Is that true, Tyler?" Riley asked.

He glanced down at the boy. "Knowing horses, I'd say Beth was being straight with you. But if you don't believe her, you need to get to know some of the horses at the Second Chance and then discover it for yourself. Prince Charming has his moments."

"You're teasing me, right?"

"I promise you, I'm telling the truth," Beth reassured him. "I remember one time when my brother Zach blew out the side of our barn with his high school experiment."

Riley's eyes widened. "Huh?"

"It was for his junior chemistry entry in the science fair. Well, it went wrong and he blew out the side of the barn. Spooked my horse and she charged out of the barn. It took us two days to round up all the animals and for me to find Milly. She was so mad at Zach that she never let him near her again. Can't say I blamed her."

Amazingly, both Tyler and Riley laughed. The sound made her heart sore.

"My dad didn't think it was so funny." She joined the guys in their laughter until tears ran down her cheeks. She wiped them away. "Didn't your brother do anything stupid like that?" The instant that last word fell from her mouth, Beth realized her mistake.

The joy and laughter in the cab evaporated. Riley sobered and glanced at Tyler, then stared down at the fried pie in his hands.

This time the tears in Beth's eyes were from pain.

Lord, give me the words to comfort. Taking a deep breath, she said, "I am sorry, Riley. I didn't mean—I know you loved your brother."

He didn't look at her, but nodded.

How could such a warm, fun atmosphere instantly change? Beth stole a glance at Tyler. Every muscle in the man's body had gone tight. Riley's pain washed over Tyler. So not only had she wounded Riley, but Tyler, too.

There were no words to make it right, so she remained quiet, praying.

When they arrived at the ranch, Susan stood beside her new SUV. Zach and Sophie chatted with her.

Beth wanted to say something to Riley, but no words came to mind. She opened her door and slipped out of the truck, allowing Riley to exit. He walked to his mom's vehicle.

"Did you have a good time, son?" Susan asked coming toward them.

He shrugged and got into his mother's car.

When the woman turned back to Tyler, Beth introduced herself. "Riley had an amazing day. He helped me with one of the horses, was the side walker for a young girl and ate all his dinner and the rest of my onion rings. And devoured a cherry fried pie."

"Terrific." Susan's face lighted with delight.

"I was telling Riley about my brother blowing up our barn with his high school chemistry experiment." She looked at Zach standing behind Susan and saw his surprise. "When we finished laughing, I asked Riley—" tears choked Beth's throat "—if his brother did anything like that." Beth bit her lips. "I instantly realized my mistake. I'm sorry." Tears slipped from the outside corners of her eyes.

A sad smile filled Susan's face and she grasped Beth's hand. "Thank you for telling me about Riley's progress. He was close to his brother, especially after my husband was killed in a car accident when Riley was in the first grade. His older brother tried to fill the gap left in Riley's life."

Each word made Beth more miserable. "I am so sorry."

Susan squeezed Beth's hand and drew her close. "Thank you for helping him." When Susan pulled back, she wiped her own tears away. She turned to

Tyler and brushed a kiss across his check. "You've been a blessing."

She walked to the driver's door. "I'll call you later, Tyler, and we'll see about the schedule for next week."

"Okay."

Susan climbed into her car and pulled away from the ranch.

Beth looked from her brother and sister-in-law to Tyler. She turned and walked into the barn. She needed to be alone with her pain.

Tyler stood planted to the ground. He felt like he'd just been through a firefight on the streets of Baghdad. How had the silly, fun night turned so deadly and emotional in an instant?

Sophie walked to his side. "I'll go talk to her."

Tyler knew Sophie would understand how to comfort Beth, but somehow that felt cowardly. "No, I'll do it."

When Sophie started to object, Zach grasped her hand and pulled her toward the house.

"But, but—" she sputtered.

Zach leaned in and whispered something. Whatever it was, she didn't push her objections, but walked with her husband to the house.

Tyler faced the barn. He knew how to clear a house of hostiles, but he was completely clueless as to how to handle a weeping woman, and if he had his choice, he'd choose the hostiles. What did one say? I know you didn't mean the stupid thing you said?

That wouldn't work.

It was an innocent remark.

That was it. He'd go with that line of thinking.

As he walked in the barn, he thought about praying, but it was shallow and two-faced only to talk to God when he needed a favor. But lately he found himself needing to talk to God more and more.

Once inside the structure, he didn't hear any crying. Was that a good or bad sign?

Slowly he walked down the first aisle as if he was walking through a minefield. When he approached Charming's stall, he saw Dogger lying before it, then Beth inside. She stood with her face pressed into Charming's neck. She turned her head to the side and she rubbed the horse's neck with her cheek.

"I didn't mean to," she whispered to the big gelding. The horse's ears twitched.

"I know you didn't," Tyler answered.

She didn't raise her head. "But I still hurt him." Agony laced her voice.

Although his heart ached, Tyler couldn't deny it.

"I was trying so hard."

"I think you did a lot of good work with him today. I saw him laugh for the first time."

She lifted her head from the horse's neck. "Really?"

"Yeah. Cut yourself some slack."

As the words finished ringing through the barn, they pinched him, too, as he realized the words were meant for him.

She finger-combed Charming's mane then moved away from the horse. "I can understand why Riley took his brother's death so hard." She leaned against the half-wall of the stall.

"Paul told me about trying to fill the void their dad's death left in Riley's life." He rested his forearms on the top edge of the stall. "Paul was a great guy and went to all Riley's little league games. It was tough when he had his own games, but they worked it out. Riley attended Paul's games." The sadness and guilt of Paul's death washed over him.

"He was more than just someone in your unit."

"Yeah." He fell silent. "We had a lot of things in common. We both lost our fathers and struggled. Paul and I became good friends." They didn't sit with each other and spill their guts, but there was a quiet understanding between them. Paul didn't have to be guarded around Tyler and vice versa. It was a special camaraderie he had with few people. He knew that Paul would be grateful for the help he offered Riley. But the pain of the loss was an open wound.

Beth slipped her fingers through his. Those small, strong fingers became a lifeline for him. He knew she shared his pain. Gazing into her eyes, he saw a quiet understanding. She didn't try to offer him any words of comfort or try to have him analyze his feelings, but accepted him. Wounds and all.

"Thank you."

"For what?"

"For understanding. You didn't blame me and…" She nodded her head and pulled her hand from his. She gave Charming a pat. Dogger sat at her feet. She knelt and stroked the dog's head. "You're a lucky dog to have a good master."

Tyler hid his surprise at her comment, but his heart eased.

Beth stood. "I'll see you on Thursday afternoon. I'm helping Chelsea. I'll pray that Riley will want to help with her again."

He nodded. As he watched Beth walk to her car, confusion filled his brain. Dogger whined.

"What?"

The dog's soulful eyes pierced Tyler's heart. He wanted to ignore the emotions that this evening had wrung out of him—that he'd spent the past year avoiding. How had Beth turned his comforting her to her comforting him?

"I was nice to her."

The dog turned his head and looked in the direction where Beth had driven away.

Somehow, Tyler understood the longing in Dogger's eyes. Beth made things inside him shift. What was happening?

Beth fixed herself a cup of hot tea and walked out onto the balcony outside her kitchen. Her apartment was above a shop in an old part of the city. The adobe buildings dated from the late 1800s, but within the past few years, the old buildings had been revitalized and young people had started to buy up the apartments created above the stores. The apartment was close to the main downtown store, which housed the buyers for McGill and Montoya Department Stores where she worked.

"Lord, what did I do?" she quietly asked. Her cell phone rang. Beth walked into the kitchen and searched through her purse. The phone went to voice mail. Looking at the screen, she saw Sophie had called.

Beth didn't want to talk to anyone. Not yet.

They'd made progress today. Riley had snapped out of his funk with a little tough love. Tyler had opened up beyond her wildest dreams. They laughed at dinner. They laughed in the truck at her stories of Zach's adventure. That is until she put an end to it with her question about his brother.

Her phone rang. Sophie again. Beth knew her ex-roommate well enough that Sophie wouldn't stop until the phone was answered. Might as well face the music now. Beth grabbed her cell. "Hello."

"I'm glad you finally answered."

Beth grimaced. "I knew you weren't going to quit until you talked to me."

"Are you okay?"

All of Beth's irritation evaporated. "I felt so bad, Sophie. You should've seen Riley's face when I asked about his brother. I didn't mean…"

"Of course you didn't. I've known you since college and never have you said anything cruel to anyone. I saw that boy with Chelsea this afternoon. Riley was into it. He made sure no one saw him, but when he knew the coast was clear his shoulders went up and he smiled. So don't give up. If I recall, you were the one who dragged Zach to Second Chance, too."

Beth knew from the first time Sophie and Zach met at her parents' ranch they were right for each other. Zach had stepped into the ranch kitchen dripping wet from the rain and clapped eyes on Sophie and stopped dead. They spent that weekend avoiding each other, but Beth knew there was chemistry between them. She tried all through college to get them back together. It was only after both of them had left the Army that they were brought together again by Zach's injury. "Thanks, Sophie."

"You pray for that boy. God can do for him what you can't."

Sophie's words eased her heart.

After they said goodbye, Beth hung up.

Beth knew Sophie hit close to the truth. It was just that Beth saw so clearly how to help others and wanted that change to happen instantly. She knew that wasn't reasonable and knew God's timing had to be there, but the waiting was *so* hard.

Her brothers had often complained about her meddling, claiming she was butting in. But more often than not, they had to admit her advice was right on the mark and if they'd followed what she said, it would've saved them grief. Too bad that wonderful ability didn't apply to her own life. It would've spared her a lot of pain.

A pain that not even her parents knew about.

Chapter Five

Tyler walked toward the open stable doors, thinking he might persuade Riley to move from his spot outside the stable entrance. Riley hadn't said much since his ride had dropped him off at the ranch. Any hope that the kid had gotten over his mood was dashed when he parked himself on the bench.

As he went about his chores, Tyler knew Riley's attitude was a test to see if those who accepted him the last time would accept him again even with his bad attitude. He'd run that routine on each set of foster parents he'd had. Amazingly, his last foster mother had ignored his bad mood and pushed and pulled him. The first weekend he was with the Olaskys, his foster mother announced she expected him to be dressed and ready for church at 8:45 a.m. on Sunday morning. He tested her, and she dragged him to church in his ripped jeans and paint-splattered T-shirt. After she walked him up to his Sunday School room and he peered inside, she whispered if he wanted to change, she'd brought his Sunday clothes and they were in the car. It didn't take him long to change and go into class. If anyone saw him in his ratty clothes no one said anything. She didn't try to change his attitude but he had to follow her rules.

Maybe Riley needed a little push. He started out of the stables, but saw Ollie standing beside Riley.

"I need some help," Ollie said.

"I don't work here."

Gazing from the top of Riley's head to his toes, Ollie took stock of the young man. "That's not what I asked you. Stand up. I need help."

Riley's eyes narrowed. When he opened his mouth to reply, Beth walked out of the office. "Good, Ollie, I was just looking for you."

Ollie glanced over his shoulder. "I'm here volunteering this young man to help me. He's got nothing better to do but warm this bench."

Riley's stance tightened.

Beth wrapped her arm around the kid's shoulders. "I was hoping he'd help me with Dusty. I wanted to saddle him for our newest rider, Captain Brenda Kaye. I thought I'd see if he remembered what to do." She turned to Riley. "Think you could pull the tack for Dusty? It should be marked in the tack room."

Riley's panicked eyes moved from Beth to Ollie. "Yeah, I think so."

"Prove it."

Riley didn't wait around but headed inside the stables. The boy wouldn't meet Tyler's gaze but walked past him. Tyler turned his attention back to Beth and Ollie.

"I couldn't stand it." Ollie pointed to the bench. "He needed to get off his backside and bad attitude."

Beth laughed. "It's that diplomat in you coming out, friend."

The older man scowled.

She slipped her arm through Ollie's and grinned. "How are you feeling today? You are looking stronger, and that ornery attitude is returning."

"I'm going to the hospital this afternoon. They're going to do the final test to see if they got it all."

"That's wonderful." Leaning up, she kissed his check. "I'll pray that you get a clean bill of health and if you do, I think we need to celebrate."

His old gnarled hand squeezed Beth's. "I knew you were a special girl that first day when you dragged your cantankerous brother here. A girl who loved others."

Beth's cheeks flamed pink. She patted his hand and whispered something in his ear. The old man laughed. "Get out of here." Tyler pried his eyes away and went to the stables.

She rushed into the stables and stopped short when she saw Tyler. "At least I didn't mow into you this time."

"It's an improvement."

"But you have to stop loitering around inside the stables if you don't want people running into you."

He shook his head, a smile curving his lips. "How do you figure it's my fault if you don't look?"

She pointed to the spot where he stood. "You're standing in traffic's way."

Was she serious? He opened his mouth to respond, but Riley said, "I think I've got it."

The boy stopped and his head came up. He stared at them. He looked ready to bolt.

"Let me see." Beth didn't look at Tyler, but walked to Riley.

"It looks like you got everything. Okay, let's find Dusty and get him ready. Our rider is a very special lady. She is an Army captain."

"So you're getting more soldiers?"

"We are. You know my brother lost…"

Their voices faded as the pair disappeared from view.

"She's a talented lady," Ollie commented. "I'm thinking she could charm the ornery out of any ass."

Tyler raised his brow.

"The four-legged kind," Ollie snapped.

"I was thinking the same thing myself."

Ollie rubbed the back of his neck. "That kid's got a big chip on his shoulder."

Tyler opened his mouth to defend Riley, but Ollie raised his hand. "Don't thank me. I was just trying to get him doing something besides stewing. When you're working, you don't feel so sorry for yourself." He stomped off to the far aisle.

Well, at least Tyler didn't need to offer a response to Ollie's comment. As Tyler went back to work, he found himself wanting to talk to Beth about how she got Riley to talk to her. Maybe he could follow her technique.

Beth sat with her brother and sister-in-law at the dinner table. Tyler had been invited to join them, but made excuses.

They talked over how the session with Captain Kaye had gone. She'd been in a market in Baghdad meeting an Iraqi contact when the bomber, a young man, blew himself up. "Well, I at least got Riley to help me saddle Dusty for her. I think he secretly took pride in his accomplishment."

"Ease up on yourself," Sophie said. "You're not perfect."

"Amen to that," Zach piped in.

Sophie glared at her husband. "We all make mistakes. And I think that Riley is going to recover. He certainly seemed to improve by the time he left, and he made a big hit with the captain before she left."

"She told Riley he reminded her of her nephew."

Sophie walked over to the stove and brought the pan of brownies to the table. She cut everyone a piece. She devoured hers. "Zach, would you get me a glass of milk?"

Zach stopped mid-chew, jumped up and poured Sophie a glass of milk. He brought both the glass and the milk jug to the table.

Setting the filled glass and jug in front of Sophie, he said, "In case you want a second glass."

Beth's nearly fell out of her chair at her brother's action. She remembered when she had the flu and asked her brother for a 7-UP. He stood at her bedroom door and bellowed to his mother that she wanted a drink.

"What that young man needs," Sophie said between sips of milk, "is to be around other kids his own age."

Sophie's comment brought Beth to the present.

"You okay?" Sophie asked.

Beth shook off the memory, but Sophie's comment had sparked an idea. "What if we invited Riley to go on the lock-in with our youth group next week?"

Sophie sat back. "That's a brilliant idea. What do you think, Zach?"

He cut himself another brownie and poured a second glass of milk for himself. "That could work," he mumbled around his brownie.

"Do you think that Riley's mom will go for that idea?" Sophie asked.

"She'll love anything that will cause her son to laugh and be young." The more Beth thought about it, the more excited she became. All three of the McClure kids had done lock-ins when they were teens. Those times were some of her best memories from high school.

"Riley's mom might agree, but do you think that Riley will feel comfortable enough to spend the night with teens he doesn't know?" Sophie asked.

"That could be a problem," Beth admitted. But it was such a good idea that— "What if I ask Tyler if he wants to help chaperone the night along with me? There'd be two people he'd know. Besides, I have a sneaking suspicion that Tyler needs a night of fun."

Laughing, Sophie pointed with the remains of her brownie. "Oh, you're sneaky."

"You don't know the half of it," Zach muttered.

"No, I'm not sneaky," Beth protested.

Zach's brow shot up.

But Beth couldn't hide her smile. "What I am is creative. And determined."

"Like when you dragged me to your house to

meet your brother?" Sophie took the last bite of Zach's brownie. Zach didn't object.

Beth grinned unrepentantly. "I can't help it that you two were so attracted to each other the instant you saw each other, I thought you'd blow out the electric panel in the house."

Both Zach and Sophie blushed.

"You're nuts, sis," Zach replied, covering his face.

Sophie turned to her husband. "You did avoid me that weekend."

"What?"

Beth stood. "I think I'll take Tyler a brownie and float the idea by him." She cut two large pieces out of the pan and wrapped them in a napkin. "Wish me luck."

"I hope you treat him better than you do your own brother," Zach shouted after her as she left the kitchen.

Beth laughed. A knock sounded at the front door.

"Maybe I won't have to seek him out." Beth walked to the front door. She opened it and found Ollie. "Hey, Ollie, come in." She stepped back. A moment of fear shot through her. "Is everything okay?"

Zach and Sophie appeared in the living room.

The quiet man took off his hat. "I wanted to share my news with you since you're family."

Beth held her breath.

"My doc gave me a clean bill of health. I am well."

Beth, being the closest, got to the older man first and wrapped her arms around his shoulders, then kissed him on the cheek.

He blushed.

Sophie next hugged him, followed by Zach's handshake.

"Well, we need to mark the occasion. I have some ice cream and brownies. Let's celebrate."

They all gathered in the kitchen. Ollie looked uncomfortable, but Beth knew that the old man didn't have any family left here in the state. Sophie and Zach had adopted him as an honorary uncle.

"Have you told Margaret?" Sophie asked. Margaret had owned the ranch before Sophie and Zach. After she suffered a stroke, she sold the ranch to Sophie.

"No. I thought I'd go by her place tomorrow morning."

Everyone took a bite of brownie and celebrated Ollie's good news.

"How's Tyler working out?" Zach asked.

"He's coming along. Works hard. He doesn't need me to hold his hand and tell him what to do."

Beth knew that was high praise from the old man.

"'Course, that dog of his is a prickly critter."

After he took another bite of his brownie, he added, "But that dog's a smart one."

After they finished their brownies and ice cream, Ollie left. Beth walked out with him. She watched as he got in his truck and drove away before she walked down to the foreman's house. The cool night surrounded her as she thought of the best way to approach Tyler about helping at the lock-in. She didn't want to think of why the idea of having Tyler help that night was so compelling. She was helping Riley, she told herself. It had nothing to do with the tall man who had brownish-green eyes that held some secret.

The front door of the foreman's house stood open and, through the screen door, Beth could see the living room furniture. No television sounds floated out of the house, but the notes of a guitar filled the air. Did he have the radio on?

"Tyler," she called out, lightly knocking on the screen door's wooden frame.

Dogger appeared in the living room. He disappeared and a moment later Tyler walked to the door. His eyes questioned her. "Is something wrong?"

"No." Raising the napkin, she showed him the brownies. "I thought you might like some dessert."

He unlatched the screen and opened the door. She slipped by him and moved into the kitchen.

He followed her. "You seem to know your way around this house. Did you ever live here?"

"No, but when Sophie was running this ranch before she and Zach married, I spent a lot of time in this house." She placed the brownie on the table and sat. "I hope you like chocolate."

As he looked at the brownies, she witnessed the transformation of his expression from bland into a stunning smile. It forced the air from Beth's lungs.

"I do. The Army always kept us well supplied with chocolate."

She gathered her scattered wits. "Good. I thought you might eat these while I run an idea by you."

"Oh."

"Relax, I'm not going to ask you to the homecoming game."

The joke didn't go over well. His face lost all traces of humor and he sat across from her, stone-faced again.

She signed. "Sorry. I guess I shouldn't try to go into stand-up comedy."

That brought the reaction she wanted. His lips twitched. "Good idea. Okay, let's hear it." He picked up a brownie.

"Next Sunday night our church is going to have what we call an all-night lock-in. The teens gather at the church at 6:00 p.m. Then they spend the night doing fun things like swimming, bowling, a pizza party and going to a game arcade. I think that is just the perfect thing for Riley. He could be with kids his age and maybe develop some friendships and be a kid. Our youth pastor oversees the entire event. Of course, there are adult volunteers who go with the kids to chaperone." She glanced up at Tyler. His expression was measured, revealing nothing.

"When Zach, Ethan and I were teenagers, the lock-in was the highlight of our summers. It's the grand party before school begins. And it was a great excuse to stay up all night. It also gave us bragging rights when we went back to school."

Tyler demolished the first brownie in two bites. He wasn't kidding about liking chocolate. He started the second one.

"So what do you think? Would Susan let her son go to the lock-in?"

It took three bites to finish the second one. Beth went to the cabinet and pulled out a glass. Opening the refrigerator, she looked for the milk. A quart sat on the bottom shelf. She held it up. He nodded. After she poured him a glass, she gave it to him.

After he downed the milk, he studied her. "Why do you want to do this for Riley?"

The man didn't give his trust lightly, did he? "Because I see a young man who could use a friend and I want to help."

Sitting back in the chair, Tyler studied her. She knew he was trying to guess her motives.

"My heart goes out to that young man, and I think he just needs to be a teenager and have fun," she explained. "He might find a friend. If you haven't already noticed, Riley's starting to blossom, in spite of my flub."

His gaze ran over her face. "I've noticed."

"Well, I think this lock-in is a golden opportunity. Other teens could reach Riley better than you or I."

He wasn't convinced.

"And," she grudgingly admitted, "my brothers always tease me about being the Dear Abby of Albuquerque, but there's something in me that can't stand to see Riley closed up like that." Her voice thickened with emotion.

"I went to several lock-ins when I was a teen, so I know what they are."

He was talking, which was a good sign.

"And wasn't it a good experience?"

"The first time my foster parents wanted me to go, I didn't know what to think. I was suspicious that they'd let me stay out all night."

Excitement ran through Beth's veins. "Did you have fun?"

"Yeah, but Riley wouldn't know any of the kids."

"But I'd be there and you could be there, too."

He sat up. "What?"

"Pastor needs a couple more chaperones, and your being an ex-soldier would be perfect. Dealing with teenagers should be a piece of cake compared to what you went through."

His eyes narrowed. "Very nicely done."

Her cheeks grew warm.

"Do you play chess, too?"

The man nailed her. Saw through her maneuvering. A smile danced around her mouth, and she looked out the windows into the night. "It would help Riley."

He rubbed his chin. "You fight dirty, lady."

She reached across the table and grabbed his hand. "It works on so many levels, Tyler."

He glanced down at their hands, then back at her.

Beth blushed and pulled her hand back and went on. "Riley could meet some friends at church. I'm sure Susan would love that, and you can have time with him away from here. You could let me beat you at some video games."

"Don't count on it. I don't throw games. I learned quickly in foster care that I had to win to make it in the places where I was."

"Then I can tell Pastor you and I will go with the kids and we'll have another teen?"

Tyler shook his head and laughed. That laughter resonated in her soul.

"I know when I've been outmaneuvered. You can count on me if Riley agrees."

Wanting to do a little victory jig, Beth tried to hide her excitement. "Do you want me to talk to Riley's mom or do you want to do that?"

"I'll let you talk to Susan. I'll work on Riley."

Beth knew when to retreat. She'd won the skirmish. "I won't impose on you anymore." She stood and headed for the front door.

He followed. "I saw Ollie's truck earlier."

"You should've come up. He came to tell us he's cancer-free."

"That is good news."

At the screen Beth turned and listened to the silence.

"What?"

"I thought I heard a guitar earlier."

He didn't say anything.

She raised up on her tiptoes and brushed a kiss across his cheek. "Thanks. You won't regret it. I think you'll see a change in Riley." She pushed open the door. "And pray. God can do things that we can't even imagine."

Dogger slipped out onto the porch. Beth scratched his head. "Keep guard on your master," she whispered. At her car, she flashed Tyler a thumbs-up, then slipped into the front seat.

As she drove home, Beth's heart sang. Too bad

Tyler didn't flash that smile more often. It certainly packed a wallop.

Of course, the last man whose smile was that potent turned out to be a monster.

Tyler walked outside and leaned against the porch pillar. Dogger looked up at him.

"She's quite a whirlwind, isn't she, boy?"

Dogger looked back at the driveway.

"How'd she do that?" Tyler couldn't help but admire Beth for her skilled strategy of getting him to agree to chaperone a bunch of teens on an all-night lock-in. The woman had talent. One instant he was eating home-baked brownies, a treat he hadn't had since he left home close to a year ago, and the next instant he'd agreed to take Riley to the lock-in.

The woman would make a fine general. She could see the field and her tactical moves were perfect. He didn't see the trap until she sprang it on him. Keep an eye on a group of teenagers. What could he do? The opportunity for Riley to have fun appealed to him and she had to know he'd do anything for the kid.

The few lock-ins he attended as a teen were some of the best times he had in high school. The lock-in his senior year a couple of friends fell asleep and the other teens dyed their hair purple with his help. He grinned at the memory.

Good memories were something Riley needed. Paul would want that for his little brother.

The big question now was, could he convince Riley? He had no doubt that Beth would talk Susan into the idea.

"So did Beth convince you to go to the lock-in?" Zach stood on the sidewalk before the ranch manager's house.

"Yeah, I walked straight into that trap. You think I might be able to get out of it?"

Zach moved up the walk and leaned against the porch pillar supporting the roof. "Not a chance. And you can assume that Beth will get Susan to agree."

"That's what I thought. And I'll get to spring the idea on Riley."

Zach shook his head. "I've been on the short end of Beth's schemes many a time. And, of course, Ethan has more stories than I do."

"So you're saying I'm outmanned."

"You got it. But Beth's idea is a good one. Be prepared to run a hard race that night. I suggest a nap before you go. Teenagers are ingenious and you'll need the extra energy."

"Are you going?" Tyler asked.

The grin that split Zach's face told Tyler all he needed to know. "My wife's pregnant and neither of us needs to be up all night. But take heart. Ollie and I will take over your chores that Monday."

"Thanks," Tyler grumbled.

"No need to thank me." Zach turned and walked back to the main house.

Looking up into the night sky, Tyler studied the stars. With the elevation of Albuquerque, the stars shone so brightly it was as if Heaven smiled down on him, telling him to rest. He sat on the top step. Dogger settled beside him. Tyler felt as if God was whispering to him to come home.

Come home.

Tyler let the feeling settle around him and he felt a peace he hadn't experienced in a long time.

Chapter Six

The next morning, Beth prayed as she punched in the last digit of Susan Carter's cell phone into her phone. By the fourth ring Beth's anxiety had grown. She needed to talk to Susan before Tyler could approach Riley.

"Susan Carter." Her voice reflected a woman of strength.

"Susan, this is Beth McClure."

A long pause, followed by, "Is there something wrong with Riley?"

"No, no, nothing like that."

"Oh."

"I want to ask you if I might take Riley to the lock-in our church is having next Sunday night." Beth went on to explain the event. "I think it would be good for Riley to be with kids his own age and it would be a night for him to be a carefree kid."

Silence settled on the line. Beth started to panic. What could she say to ease Susan's anxiety?

Finally a sound came from Susan's end. It sounded like a choked cry.

Beth's stomach lurched with fear. Oh, what had she done? "Susan, I didn't mean to offend."

"No," came the tear-filled response. "No, you didn't offend me. I'm just overwhelmed with gratitude. I think your idea is marvelous. It's just the thing Riley needs. We've only been in Albuquerque for six months. My company transferred me down here and gave me a good raise. I thought it would help us both to have a fresh start away from old memories. Riley felt like I was abandoning Paul and his dad by leaving Kansas City." She stopped, and Beth heard Susan trying to speak though her tears. "That's why Tyler's showing up in our lives has been a such a blessing. Riley has an adult male in his life who knew Paul."

Beth's heart eased. "Well, boys are kinda funny. Everyone claims that girls are impossible as teens, but I have two older brothers, and they run girls a race for being impossible. I think Riley will like the youth group. Our youth pastor is a wonderful man who has a gift for reaching teens. He listens, talks to them, but doesn't allow any nonsense. Wrong's wrong, and he tells them so. Amazingly, the teens love him, knowing where they stand."

"Sounds like the kind of person to help. It's okay with me, but what if Riley doesn't want to go?"

"Don't worry. I'm going to let Tyler float the idea to Riley. And Tyler has volunteered to chaperone, along with me, that night."

"That's wonderful."

"And you're welcome to go to church with us Sunday morning to check out the church and pastors," Beth offered, hoping to ease any fears Susan might have.

"I like that idea. Riley can meet the pastor and kids and so can I."

After hanging up, Beth dialed Second Chance Ranch. Sophie put the call through to the stables.

"What?" Ollie demanded, answering the phone.

"Ollie, you're going to have to cut back that charm."

He growled and she laughed, glad to have the cranky man back.

"Would you please put Tyler on the phone?"

The man didn't reply to her but bellowed for Tyler. Beth had to yank the phone away from her ear. After a couple of minutes, Tyler came on.

"Tyler, Susan gave our plan a go. Now the ball's in your court."

"Okay." He hung up.

Tyler ran a second to Ollie in telephone manners. Beth slowly hung up the phone on her desk.

"Thank You, Lord." Looking around, Beth wanted to hop up and dance. It was a victory for Riley. And Tyler. He needed this time to laugh as much as Riley did. And she wanted that for him, as well.

But in her heart, she knew she wanted to spend the time with Tyler—and Riley, she hastily reassured herself.

"Beth," Jill Kempa, Beth's boss called out as she walked out of her office. "I need you to go to Tuba City and take a contract to David Santos. He's finally decided to start using our stores to distribute his jewelry and handbags. And he agreed to an exclusive."

David Santos, a brilliant but erratic artist, had developed the hottest new line of Southwestern jewelry and handbags. The extraordinary artisan had an eye for materials and how things should be put together. She'd discovered his small store when she drove through the Hopi and Navajo reservations, looking for local jewelry, clothing and purses with a Southwestern flair. She'd developed a friendship with him and had tried to get him to distribute his merchandise line through their stores. He didn't want anything to do with it. The last time she had talked to him was right after Christmas last year.

"But—"

"He specified that you bring him the contract."

How could she take him the contract and be back in time for the lock-in? "Couldn't we just fax the contract to him?" Beth cringed the instant the words left her mouth. She held up her hand. "I'll go home and pack now."

"My secretary's made the travel arrangements. We've chartered a plane. Pick up the information at her desk." Jill marched out of the room.

Great news, but David's timing sucked. Couldn't he have decided to go with them next week? Or two weeks ago, instead of days before the lock-in?

Jill paused at the door to the large room that housed purchasing. "You'd better hurry. The plane leaves in ninety minutes."

As she threw things in her purse, she prayed, *It's in Your hands, Lord. I know You'll guide everything, but I would've liked to be here.*

Then Beth laughed, because she knew He could handle it.

"Where's Beth?" Riley asked as he walked up to the stables.

Sophie and Tyler stood by the mounting steps, checking out Charming's tack.

"She's on an unscheduled business trip," Sophie answered. "She called me as she raced to catch her plane."

"Oh." Disappointment rang in his word.

"But you can help me get Brownie ready for Chelsea," Sophie told the boy.

"I don't know. Maybe I'll just hang out front." He turned and walked down the aisle.

Tyler moved to Riley's side and lowered his voice. "I thought Paul told me you were made of sterner stuff."

Riley's chin jerked up. "You don't know anything."

"I know that not a day goes by that I don't miss him, but I think Paul would want better from you."

Riley's chin hardened.

"I also know Paul would be proud of you for helping Chelsea. And you know he would." Tyler held his breath, praying his gamble would pay off.

Riley looked at Sophie, then back at Tyler. "Okay. I'll go get her tack."

As the boy disappeared into the tack room, Tyler let out his breath. Relief made his knees weak. He rejoined Sophie.

"I don't know what you said, but it worked."

"I'm amazed, too." But he knew that he'd had some help from above.

"Beth will be excited to learn what he did." Sophie looked out of the open door and saw Brenda Kaye. "The captain's here."

Tyler watched as Zach shook the woman's

hand. The two of them walked toward the mounting steps.

"Captain, did you get to meet Tyler Lynch the last time you rode? He is also ex-Army and will be your sidewalker."

She waved off Zach's using of her rank and held out her hand to Tyler. "Nice to meet you, Tyler. So you're going to make sure I don't slip off of the horse?"

The captain stood five foot seven, slender, but walked with a cane. Her brown hair was held back by a baseball cap, but her hazel eyes missed nothing. And in those eyes, Tyler saw pain.

Tyler nodded. "I'm going to try, ma'am."

She waved off the respectful reply. "It's just Brenda. I'm only in reserves now."

Tyler instantly liked the woman. He guessed she was the type of officer who commanded respect because of her actions.

"Do you think you'll need help mounting?" Zach asked. "And let me tell you, the first time I was here, I needed help. It didn't matter one whit that I rode all my life."

She grinned. "You're telling me not to let my pride get in the way?"

Tyler's gaze met Zach's. The lady went up several notches in his estimation.

"Yes, I am."

"Let's give it a try." She handed Tyler her cane. "I'll probably need a little steadying to get on this beast."

The woman won Tyler's respect.

Tyler found Riley with Dogger in the stables. He was brushing Brownie. He paused, amazed at the kid's actions. Beth's influence was paying dividends. He stopped by Brownie's head and gave her a pat. "I saw you with Chelsea earlier."

Riley stopped. "Yeah." He sounded unsure of himself.

"You did a great job with her and a good job saddling Brownie."

The boy's shoulders eased, but he continued to brush the horse.

"You feeling comfortable around here?"

"I guess."

Tyler read through the kid's act. He'd done the same thing when he first went to a foster home. No matter how much you like something, keep it cool. Tyler recognized the defensive ploy.

"Chelsea is doing better. I watched today and she held her posture longer."

"I saw that, too. And she knew it." Riley set the curry brush down.

"Later, you think you might like to do a little riding?"

"Really?" Riley's eyes sparkled.

Tyler laughed. "Really. I didn't ask you here only to help. You need to learn to ride."

"Yeah, that sounds okay."

"Good. There's one more rider I need to help with. After that, we'll do some riding."

"Okay."

As the kid started to turn away, Tyler stopped him. "I have something I want to ask you."

Riley stilled, wary and suspicious, but said nothing.

"Have you ever stayed up all night playing games and eating pizza?"

"What?"

His approach wasn't working. "Beth's church does what they call a lock-in."

Riley frowned. "Lock-in? What's that?"

"The teens get to spend the night doing neat stuff like golfing, bowling, playing video games and other cool stuff. And as I said before, they stay up all night and eat pizza. It's the big bash before school starts. Beth has invited you to come to the one this coming Sunday. It's a big deal they do once a year."

"What's the catch?"

"I think the church wants kids to have fun and make friends before the new school year starts."

"I've never heard of that."

"My church back in Oklahoma did it, only we

stayed at the church building and didn't get to go different places. And other churches do it, too."

Riley folded his arms across his chest. "That can't be right."

Tyler's mind searched for something to convince the kid about the event. Zach entered the stables. Tyler called him over.

"Zach, I was trying to explain to Riley about the lock-in on Sunday night. He doesn't believe me. You've been. Will you explain it to him?"

Zach laughed. "It was the best time I had in high school." He explained about his adventures and how he'd helped for a number of years. "It's something you don't want to miss."

"Zach, where are you?" Sophie called.

"Gotta go."

"Satisfied?" Tyler asked.

Riley still seemed reluctant. "Why does Beth want me to do that?"

C'mon, kid, give it up. Although Tyler wanted Riley to agree to the plan, he understood the kid's cautiousness. For a long time he'd questioned his foster parents' motives for being nice to him. "Well, Beth thought it would be fun for you. And knowing the other kids before you start school helps sometimes. I know it helped me when I met a friend my first year at the lock-in. He ended up in five of my classes. We became good friends."

Riley remained silent.

"I am also going to the lock-in. And Beth will be there, too."

"I won't know any of the kids."

"True, but Beth suggested that we both go to church with her that morning and meet some people." He hoped Beth's argument worked for Riley as well as it did with him.

"I don't know if my mom would let me," Riley finally said.

He had him, or rather Beth had him. "Beth's got that covered. She asked your mother if it was okay for you to go. She gave us the green light."

"Mom did?"

"Yes. She left the decision up to you. So, do you think you'd like to go? You could try beating me at video games. Or at miniature golf." Tyler knew Riley's skill at that.

A smile curved Riley's lips. "You want to try and beat me?"

"I can try," Tyler replied.

"You're on."

Beth drove to the Second Chance Ranch, her stomach churning. She'd just flown in this afternoon from Tuba City, Arizona. It had taken three days for David to be satisfied with the contracts. He'd asked countless questions. What would happen if this happened, or what could he do about supplies, or ten million other questions that made Beth want to tear her hair out.

It killed her to be away from Riley and Tyler. She'd kept in contact with Sophie. Sophie told her that Riley seemed excited about the lock-in and Tyler kept asking Zach questions about the event.

Of course, she knew things were out of her hands, but the week would've been easier on her if she'd been in town. Maybe God wanted Riley and Tyler to deal with each other without her interference. At least that's what she counseled herself.

She pulled into the parking lot and grabbed the bag stashed in her truck. The Friday afternoon crowd had swelled over the past few months. On the trail leading from the second ring, she saw Riley riding Brownie. Tyler rode beside him on Charming.

"Oh, my goodness," Beth breathed.

"It's a good sight, isn't it?"

Beth looked at Sophie. She must've just come out of the office, since she was munching on crackers. Beth looked back at the riders. Riley's seat was a little tense, but Brownie didn't seem to mind. "It's a joyous sight."

"Tyler promised the boy he could ride Brownie outside the ring if he helped with several of the riders. He did."

"Oh, Sophie," she breathed, her heart racing.

"On Tuesday, Riley started giving Tyler grief, so Tyler had a little chat with him. Whatever he said did the trick. Riley helped without complaining, and Tyler let him ride."

The day she left.

"And Riley's been working since." Sophie shook her head. "He worked yesterday and got to ride again. When his mom called this morning and asked if he could come today and ride, I agreed." Sophie finished the cracker she had in her hand. "The kid's eating it up. And he's even listened to Ollie."

Beth's mouth dropped open.

"And hold on to your bag, because when Susan talked to me this morning, she said she and Riley want to go with us to church Sunday morning."

The announcement nearly brought Beth to tears. "I guess I need to hurry up and change. Do you have a T-shirt I could use? I got jeans and boots, but—" She glanced down at her gauze top.

"Sure, we've just gotten in our new ranch T-shirts. C'mon, let's get you changed. You can be our first walking advertisement."

Beth followed Sophie into the office. Riley spotted her as she reached the office door and waved. She waved back at him. Tyler even nodded at her.

Sophie pulled a shirt off the shelf and handed it to Beth. The front of the shirt had a picture of a horse and underneath the words *Second Chance Ranch.* On the back, the slogan: *New Beginnings and New Horizons.*

"Impressive. Was that your idea or Zach's?"

Sophie grinned. "What do you think?"

"Yours." Beth slipped into the bathroom and changed in record time. Beth sat beside Sophie and put on her boots.

"I've got even better news for you."

Beth paused with her foot over her boot. "What's that?"

"Well, yesterday, when Chelsea showed up for her lesson and you weren't here, Tyler and Riley stepped in and worked with her."

Beth worried about the riders she missed, but knew that Sophie would find volunteers to take her place. "That's great news." Stashing her bag behind Sophie's desk, Beth raced outside. She caught up with the guys as they were walking their mounts into the stables.

Riley saw Beth first. His eyes sparkled.

"You were great." She wanted to hug him, but held back.

"Were you surprised to see me riding?" the boy asked.

"Yes. I nearly tripped over my feet when I saw Tyler and you."

The young man looked at Tyler. "He says that I'll get better and more relaxed after a few more times."

"That's right," Tyler added. "For the few times he's been on a horse, he's doing great."

Riley gave Brownie a carrot. "Did that happen the same way for you?"

Stepping closer to Brownie, Beth rubbed the horse's nose. "I don't remember. My parents put me on a horse before I could walk."

Riley's brows shot up. "Really?"

"Tell you what. How about I help you with Brownie and I'll tell you about it."

"Okay."

"See you Sunday," Beth called out as Susan and Riley drove away. She turned and threw her arms around Tyler.

His arms automatically encircled her. His eyes briefly closed. It had been a long time since he'd hugged anyone, let alone a beautiful woman. The last time he'd hugged his ex-fiancée, it had not been a loving gesture, but an obligation. This hug meant something more.

Beth pulled back and he immediately let his arms fall to his sides. She wouldn't meet his gaze. "You did an incredible job with Riley. How did he feel about going to the church lock-in?"

"I think he was disappointed at first that you weren't here to 'make' him work." He explained what happened on Tuesday afternoon. "Riley followed directions and helped. When it was his time to ride, I caught a smile, but as soon as he noticed me looking, he lost it."

Beth's right hand fisted and she jerked it down. "Yes."

He wanted to laugh at her victory gesture.

Looking at him, she smiled. "Prayer works."

He wasn't going to go that far, but he had to acknowledge God had answered his prayers for Riley.

She walked toward the fence encircling the first ring and rested her elbows on the top slat. The afternoon sun bathed her with a golden light and it danced in her hair, making it glow as if she had a halo. The wind teased his nostrils with the sweet smell of woman. "How'd you get him to agree to come to the lock-in?" She turned her head and smiled at him.

It took a moment for his brain to reengage and have her question register. Tyler moved to stand by her, resting his arms on the fence, and explained what had happened. "I even had your brother vouch for the event. Riley couldn't get his mind around a church sponsoring something that was as fun as an all-night party."

"A typical reaction. So how'd you convince him?"

"I challenged Riley to a game of miniature golf. He took me up on the offer."

"I wish I could've seen his expression."

"I threw in that both you and I were going."

She appeared pleased. "And that worked?"

He didn't want to admit it. "Yeah."

"I'm excited that both Susan and Riley are going to church with us on Sunday. I even heard you were going, too."

He pushed away from the fence. He thought about not answering her, but she deserved a response. "If I'm going to spend the night with these kids and adults, I thought it wise to meet them earlier in the day." That was the excuse he used to convince himself it wasn't a hunger for that relationship with God.

"You're going to scope out the situation?" She half turned to him, her right elbow still on the rail.

She'd read his motives correctly.

"Anyone tell you that you see too much?" he grumbled.

Humor danced in her eyes. "My brothers are constantly telling me that. Well, I think you've done an amazing job with Riley."

Beth's praise slid into his soul and touched a place he hadn't opened up in a long time. "So, are you bringing a date to the lock-in?"

As if he'd slapped her, her expression sobered. "No. This is not a date night. I've got to supervise a lot of teens, and wouldn't even think of bringing a date."

Her answer lightened his mood. He'd wondered

all week if she had a boyfriend, but refused to ask her brother. If he did, he was sure Zach would take the question the wrong way.

"Besides, that's a moot point."

"What?"

"The boyfriend issue." Her mouth closed so hard he could hear her teeth grind.

"What are you talking about?"

"Nothing. I need to help Ollie." With those words, she walked away. He had hit a sore spot with her. What had caused that reaction? Surely, Beth wouldn't have trouble attracting interested men, so why did he have the feeling that there wasn't a special man in her life?

"Leave it alone, Lynch," he muttered to himself. He didn't want to buy any more trouble than what he had.

Chapter Seven

The music flowed around Beth as she worked, putting new hay in the horses' stalls. After the first stanza, Beth joined in, singing the contemporary chorus with gusto.

She leaned close to Charming and kissed his nose, and continued to sing, her heart joyous.

She turned and saw Tyler standing in the aisle.

"Oh." She stumbled back a step and would've fallen into Charming, but Tyler grasped her hand and pulled him to his chest.

"Careful."

Looking up to him, she saw the amusement deep in his eyes.

"That thing you've got about sneaking up on people is surfacing again."

His brow arched. "There was nothing sneaky about it. I heard the radio from the parking lot and knew that wasn't what Ollie listens to—" he motioned to the radio "—that type of music. He's a little more traditional." He shrugged. "I came to investigate it."

His explanation was logical, but she still felt flustered. She'd been rejoicing, and the music had lifted her spirit. Charming had been enjoying the music and bobbing his head, too.

"Where is everyone?" Tyler asked, glancing around the stables. "I drop Riley off at his house, and come back to find the place deserted. Odd for a Thursday night."

"Ollie had a date."

Tyler's comical expression made her laugh.

"That was my reaction, too, but Ollie's going to see Margaret, the old owner of this place. She had a major stroke last year, but she's recovering and Ollie had planned on taking her to dinner."

He continued to stare at her. "You're pulling a fast one on me, right?"

"No. Ollie's a big marshmallow inside."

Tyler didn't look convinced. "I haven't seen any evidence of that."

"That's because you're new. And not a girl."

"If you say so."

She stepped close and lowered her voice. "I'll let you in on a little secret. I always thought he had a crush on Margaret."

Tyler glanced over both shoulders, then leaned

closer to Beth's ear. "Why are you whispering? You afraid the horses will overhear you?"

She turned her mouth toward his ear. "Yes. You know what gossips the horses are."

Beth wished she had a camera to capture Tyler's puzzled expression. He threw his head back and laughed. And what a glorious sound it was.

"What am I going to do with you?"

"My brothers have that reaction, too. What's up with that?"

He shook his head. "So Ollie's out. So where's your brother? Why isn't he here, helping?"

"He got carted out to look at strollers. I know he would rather have fed the stock, but he didn't get that option. I told Sophie I'd cover for him."

"Well, you and I together can get this done in just a few minutes."

"Okay."

"Will you continue to sing to the radio?"

Beth had her suspicions. "Why?"

"Because you have a nice voice and I enjoyed listening to you."

She examined his face closely to see if he was teasing her. He appeared sincere. "Okay, but only if you sing along."

"What if I don't know the words?"

"Just hum along. Charming can't hum, but he does keep time."

He stuck out his hand. "Deal."

Taking his hand, she felt the beginning callus on his palm. When he released her hand, a stab of disappointment shot through her. She shook off her silliness and went to work.

They worked together and in less than twenty minutes all the horses had been taken care of. Beth heard him hum, but he never burst out in song. She wanted to hear his voice.

Once they finished their chores, she walked into the tack room and turned off the radio. "Thanks for the help."

"That's what Zach pays me for."

He didn't take praise well. "Zach's getting a good value for his investment."

He nodded.

They walked out of the stables. Dogger followed them.

"I'm glad you're coming on Sunday morning." She turned and started toward her car.

"Beth."

She stopped, her heart suddenly beating faster, and her stomach lurched. You would've thought she was in high school from the reaction. "Yes?"

"You want to go get one of those greasy burgers that Riley loved?"

She hesitated.

"We have to eat, you and I."

It wasn't the most romantic invitation she'd ever

received. But she wasn't looking for a date, she told herself. "Okay, but I'll drive."

"Not a problem."

The tension in her stomach eased. The man didn't need to be in the driver's seat, controlling things. She didn't want to repeat the mistake of her past.

Tyler turned to Dogger. "Stay."

They climbed into her truck. As she drove away, she saw Dogger settle on the porch. The animal trusted Tyler in a way that amazed her. She glanced at him. He sat on the passenger side, relaxed and easy with her being in control of the truck. That was important to her.

Beth took a bite of her fried pie. "Oh, that is *sooo* good."

Tyler shook his head. The lady had demolished her burger and fries with gusto. She wasn't the kind of woman who nibbled her food around the edges, then complained about her weight, as his ex-fiancée endlessly had. His ex constantly worried about her weight and worked out in the gym, but he never saw her physically work as he'd witnessed Beth doing this afternoon.

Beth took another bite, but the coconut filling dribbled out of the corner of her mouth. She laughed and he reached out and caught the filling on his finger. She grabbed a napkin and wiped her mouth.

"Try it." Beth nodded to his finger with filling on it.

He licked the filling off his finger. "I can see why you like that."

She offered him her last bite. Earlier, when he'd tried to pay for her dinner and fried pie, she'd refused to allow it. He wondered at her reaction, but here she offered him the last bite. He took the last piece of pie and popped it into his mouth.

Beth wasn't wrong. That was good.

"Isn't that good?"

"You're right. And I know Riley shares your opinion."

She rested her arms on the table. "I like him. He started out as prickly as some of the cactus south of here, but that boy's got a good heart."

Tyler had to agree. Once the grief and moodiness lifted off of Riley's spirit, his personality had come out. The kid Paul talked about showed up. "Riley asked me about you. Wondered why you traveled so much."

"Did you explain I was a buyer for M&M?"

"I did, but I don't think he can imagine it. He said the store sounds like the candy. M&M."

"We get that a lot. The store's full name is McMill and Montoya." Beth's fingers played with the moisture from her tea glass on the table top. "I have an idea." She looked up at him. "Why don't you two come by the store tomorrow afternoon? There are some great sales for the start of school and Riley can shop. And you can buy a couple of shirts, too."

"Are you saying that I look bad in my T-shirts and jeans?"

"I kind of wonder what you'd look like in a dress shirt and pants." Oddly, he wanted to squirm. He had nice clothes. At the house in Oklahoma City. And his uniform.

"Riley probably needs new clothes for school. Or we can use the excuse of getting a cool shirt for the lock-in."

Tyler liked that idea. "Okay. I think Susan was complaining that she needed to take Riley shopping for some new clothes for school."

"Then we've got a date tomorrow afternoon. Tell one of the cashiers when you get to the store to call the purchasing office and tell them who you are and you're at the store. They will let me know."

A date.

The words stood out like a neon sign. A date.

He liked that idea. "Sounds like a plan."

Beth heard from Tyler around two-forty. Both Susan and Riley liked the idea of shopping for new school clothes. The boys were on their way to the store. She came down from the fifth floor to wait for them. Yesterday, having Tyler help her with the stock, then going for burgers, had been the most fun she'd had in a long time. When he'd offered to buy her dinner, she'd refused, not wanting the pleasant afternoon to end in a "date." It made her uncomfortable.

Why? she found herself asking, but each time the thought came up, she pushed it aside. She wasn't willing to examine the why. Instead, she buried herself in paperwork, using the excuse that it needed to be done before the lock-in. It was a thin excuse, but she wasn't complaining.

She walked through the men's department, thinking of things that would look good on Tyler and Riley.

"Beth."

She froze at the sound of that voice from the past. She didn't need to turn around to know who'd called out to her. At one time, his was the voice she loved hearing. She turned, coming face to face with Gavin Humphrey, her ex-boyfriend. The man who had slapped her.

He was still handsome, with brownish-blond hair that curled on the ends when it grew too long, deep blue eyes and dimples when he smiled. He looked a little worse for wear. He had put on about twenty pounds, and his once sparkling eyes were now flat and dull.

"Hello, Gavin."

They were words she never thought she'd utter again. They sounded rusty, being dredged from some place deep inside her soul.

"How are you?" he asked. He stood on the other side of the table displaying dress shirts.

"Well." She didn't have anything she wanted to say to him.

"Is that all you have to say to me after all this time?"

A rage rose up in her and she wanted to throw something at him, but that wasn't an option. Instead, she looked at the shirt he had in his hand. "Those are on sale. With a coupon, they're twenty-five percent off."

He shook his head. "That's not what I meant."

Beth noticed he wasn't wearing a wedding ring.

"It's been a long time since we've seen each other," he added.

What an understatement.

He set the shirt down and walked around the edge of the table. Beth refused to back up.

"When I came back from my family's vacation in Europe and called, you weren't there."

She'd spent the summer with her mother's sister in Colorado, working at a dude ranch. Aunt Nancy needed an extra counselor/hand and when she'd called, Beth had jumped at the chance.

"I haven't seen you since our prom night."

And there was a reason for that. "The register for the men's department is over in the back corner." She turned away, but his hand shot out, catching her.

She stared down at the offending hand. She wasn't going to play his game. "Let go." When she looked up, his eyes narrowed. She'd seen that expression countless times before. Obviously, the man hadn't changed over the past ten years. Well, she had, and she wasn't going to let him intimidate her.

"Hey, Beth. There are you." Riley's voice interrupted the tug-of-war between her and Gavin.

Gavin released her arm.

Tyler took in the situation and frowned. Beth welcomed Tyler's protective demeanor. "Is there a problem?"

"No." She moved away from Gavin. "The sale runs through tomorrow."

Gavin looked at Beth, then nodded and moved away, leaving the shirt.

"Who was that?" Riley asked.

"Just a guy who wanted to buy some shirts." Beth knew her explanation sounded lame. From Riley's and Tyler's expressions, neither bought it.

"I am glad you're here," Beth forced out through her stiff lips.

Riley looked around. "So this is your store?"

"Yes, this is where I work. Let me give you the tour. I know that you need some new clothes for school and we can look for those, too."

Riley grinned. "Sounds good."

Beth walked them through the store. She explained about the store and its history. They even toured the corporate offices on the fifth floor.

"So, is this your boyfriend?" her boss's secretary asked after Beth introduced Tyler and Riley.

The comment stopped all activity in the room.

"No." Beth knew her answer sounded too harsh, and she felt embarrassed. "I mean, they are friends. They work at my brother's ranch."

The woman looked from Tyler to Beth. She didn't say anything, but the look on her face said she didn't believe a single word of Beth's explanation.

Beth's boss emerged from the elevator, her cell phone in her hand. "Good, you're here." She pointed her cell at Beth. "There's a kink with David. You need to get out there. Now."

The woman started issuing orders to her secretary about calling the private plane and making other arrangements.

Beth turned to Riley and Tyler. "I'm sorry, guys. I've got to go to see about this."

"But are you going to be back in time for the lock-in?" Riley asked, a touch of anxiety in his voice.

"I'm going to do my best to get back here in time. That's the most important thing in my life."

"Okay." Riley didn't look convinced.

Neither did Tyler.

"Ah, *querida,* how good it is to see you." David walked to her side and kissed her cheeks. When she drew back, he studied her face. "What is the matter?"

"Is there really a problem with the contract, David, or is something else going on?"

"You wound me." He clutched at his chest with a dramatic flair.

Beth rolled her eyes. David might be classified as a temperamental artist, but he was a shrewd businessman.

"If I didn't know better, I'd say this was a ploy to get me here."

He shrugged his shoulders. The handsome man was only an inch taller than her five-foot-six frame, but his coal-black hair, caught with a leather throng at this neck, proved to be longer than hers. His black mustache and goatee added drama to an already chiseled face. "Would that be so bad? You are a beautiful woman, and I am a healthy man."

She suspected a motive underlying all the trips she'd made. How could she defuse this situation? *Lord, I need some wisdom here.*

"David, you are an incredible artisan, with flair and imagination, and you impress me with your talent. But you already knew that from the first time I walked into your shop and spent over five hundred dollars."

"This is true."

"But your work will always be your first love. I know that and so do you."

He grinned.

"I could never compete with your lover. I know that and don't want the heartache that would accompany loving you." She hooked her arms around his. "So, I am going to spare my heart the pain and consider you my friend." She turned to him. "My good and talented friend. You understand?"

He studied her face for several moments, then tucked a strand of her hair behind her ear. "I knew there was a reason, *querida,* why I liked you. It will break my heart, but you are right." He held up his index finger. "But I do have some questions about how my merchandise will be handled and if it can be put on *sale.*" He said the word with such distaste that Beth grinned. "I will not have it."

"I think something can be worked out with you."

"Let us do that. But before we do such boring

stuff, what is this atrocious thing you are wearing?" He motioned to what she had on.

Beth glanced down at her business suit and white shirt. "Business attire."

He wagged his index finger. "No, no. We must dress you as a beautiful woman, then we will talk business with our lawyers." He glanced over Beth's shoulder at the two men talking in the corner.

"I think, David, it would be wiser if we do business first, then I'll let you dress me in some of your wonderful creations."

Rubbing his chin, he considered her suggestions. "*Bueno.* Let us take care of the business, then I will show you how to dress as a beautiful woman."

She kissed his cheek. "Thank you."

David grinned.

Sunday afternoon, Zach walked up to the front porch of the foreman's house. He held a plate of homemade chocolate chip cookies. "I come bringing gifts."

Tyler sat on the steps, Dogger by his side. He motioned for Zach to join him on the step. Zach handed the plate to Tyler and used both hands to ease himself down on the step.

Tyler wanted to kick himself, knowing that Zach's artificial limb sometimes limited his movements. "Sorry."

Zach waved away the comment. "Don't worry. I'm here bearing a peace offering."

"Why?"

Dogger looked with hunger at the cookies. Tyler took a cookie, made sure it was free of chocolate chips, then gave a small chunk of it to the dog. Tyler downed the rest of the cookie in two bites.

"Well, Sophie was afraid the family might've overwhelmed you this morning at church, then afterward at lunch. She also worried it might be too much without Beth here to run interference."

Tyler had ridden to church with Zach and Sophie. They'd met Zach's parents and brother and Susan and Riley there at the church, and afterward went to lunch at a local restaurant.

"Sophie worried that all that McClure charm in one place might be too much for you. Of course, Susan and Riley lapped it up."

Indeed they had. In the midst of the chatter and laugher, Tyler found he missed Beth. Apparently, the issues with the contract were dragging on longer than she expected. She'd called him this morning and apologized. She'd also talked with Susan. "No, it wasn't too much."

Zach's brow arched.

"Okay, maybe it was more than I was used to, but I didn't need a flak jacket and helmet." A couple of times, though, Tyler had wanted to excuse himself and walk out back for a moment of quiet.

Laughing, Zach grabbed a cookie off the plate. "It was almost more than I could handle, and I've lived with them. Mom's coming by later to go baby shopping with Sophie. What they're going to get, I don't know. Thankfully, I won't have to go this time. Who knew there was so much baby stuff?" He took several more bites of the cookie.

Zach seemed to lead a charmed life with a family and a wife who loved him.

"You've been a big help here." Zach looked out over the corrals. "I'm thinking that over the next few months, I'm going to have to go to birthing classes and do all sorts of strange things connected with having a baby. I was hoping you'd like to stick around for a while and take up the slack. I know Ollie's been given the green light from his cancer, but he's not a spring chicken and I'd like to have some help for him." He turned his head and met Tyler's gaze.

Tyler didn't hesitate. "I'd be happy to help you out, Zach. I find myself wanting to stick around."

"Good. That takes a load off my shoulders. And I think you'll also help some of the veterans coming to the ranch. I know Captain Kaye said she'd enjoyed talking to you."

He admired the captain. She might have posed

as a health professional while in Iraq, but he knew there was more to her story.

"After I explained to her about Dogger, she told me about the dog that came around their camp and the guys fed him. Then one day, the mutt didn't show up. She wondered if he'd been killed."

"We each carry our own nightmares." Zach looked out over the corrals.

Amen to that.

A car drove up the front private drive, which ran from the parking lot by the foreman's house and main house, then to the main garage. Zach's mother jumped out and waved to him. Zach waved back.

"I gotta go. Be sure and take a nap before tonight. You're going to need it."

"You think Beth will make it home in time?"

Zach laughed. "Apparently, you don't know my sister as well as I do. She'll make it."

That eased Tyler's heart.

Tyler stretched out on the couch. Each time he closed his eyes to nap, he heard the sermon from this morning about giving God our wounds and scars and allowing Him to heal them, not letting them fester, thus making us useless to the Kingdom.

The message hit home, but he didn't know if

he could let go of the pain just yet. The pastor's words echoed Brenda's warning.

A spiritual hunger had awakened in his soul, but he wasn't quite sure how to let go of the guilt.

His mind turned to his foster parents. From the time his parents were killed, his life had been in turmoil. Sure, his grandmother had eased his heart, but there had been a big hole inside him. Grandma's death eighteen months later hadn't added to the peace in his life. And he'd acted out until he landed with the Olasky family.

He smiled at the memory.

He needed to call them. They had given him rules, but also given him an abundance of love. And they'd changed his life by taking him to church. He needed to make peace with that part of his life.

He got up and went to the phone and dialed their number. On the third ring, the phone was picked up. "Hello," his foster sister, Terri, said. "Hello."

His throat clogged up momentarily. "Hi, sis."

"Tyler. Oh, my heavens, is that you, Tyler?"

"Yes. You sound like I'm calling from the dead." The words hit him. In a way he was. "I just wanted to call and say hello."

"Oh, it's so good to hear from you. Are you all right? You're not sick or injured, are you?"

"No, just delinquent."

"That doesn't matter."

Tyler heard his foster mother ask who was on the phone.

"Mom, it's Tyler."

In the next instant the other extension picked up. "Tyler."

"Hi, Mom." It was so good to hear her voice. Margaret Olasky was the only foster mother he called "mom."

"Oh, Tyler, it's so good to hear from you. How are you? You're not hurt or anything?"

He laughed. "Terri already covered that territory. I'm fine." Margaret worried over his health, his well-being, his relationship with others. His foster father would quietly evaluate a situation, then allow him to come up with the answers on his own.

"I just thought it was time to check in."

"I'm glad."

For the next fifteen minutes he talked with his entire family, catching up on what had happened in everyone's life. "I'm going to be in Albuquerque for a while, Mom, helping a fellow veteran with his equine therapy ranch."

"That's wonderful," his foster father said. "What do you do?"

After another fifteen minutes of explaining about the ranch, Tyler said, "I just wanted to give you a heads-up." He gave them the phone number.

"I love you, son," his mother added.

The blessing settled over his spirit. "Thank you for understanding. I'll talk to you later." When he hung up, his heart felt light.

Maybe he was on the right road.

Chapter Eight

When Beth drove up to the church Sunday evening, she spotted the buses waiting on the far side of the parking lot. She was later than she'd wanted to be. David Santos, the company lawyers and guys in distribution had hammered out the kinks in the contracts with her mediation. Sales on his merchandise would only happen when and if he okayed it. When they went to fly out early this morning, the charter plane had developed a fuel line problem. It had taken most of the day to fix it, but they did and flew back into the city about five-thirty. Beth drove directly from the airport to the church. She still sported her sandals, tiered peasant skirt and bright pink T-shirt with a thick leather belt that David insisted she wear to show off his line of clothing and leather goods.

She'd planned on being early to talk with the youth pastor about Tyler and Riley, but obviously that wasn't to be. She had the oddest feeling that the delay served Heaven's purpose.

She'd missed going to church with everyone this morning and worried about how things had gone. She'd called Sophie and asked for an update. According to Sophie, Susan and Riley seemed to enjoy the service, but Tyler wasn't comfortable. Why?

Parking the car, she scrambled out and walked to their unique building. The church had bought a bankrupt store and converted it into a church. Since then, buildings had been added, and a new sanctuary had been built. They now had beautiful stained glass in the new sanctuary. The old building had been converted into classrooms and a gym.

Teens and their parents were milling around the entrance to the older building. Two tables were set up inside the door for the kids and their parents to check in.

Several of the teens shouted out greetings. She waved and smiled at them, trying to tamp down the worry riding her. Where were Riley and Tyler?

"Hey, Beth, how are you?" Mike Neils, the youth pastor, asked.

"Late, but grateful to be here."

He frowned at her outfit. "Are you going to be able to bowl in that?"

She glanced down at her clothes. "No. I raced

from the airport to get here. I've got a change of clothes in my car. Are you ready to tackle the youth tonight?"

"I am."

"Are my guys here yet?" *Her guys?* The words shocked Beth. Since when did she think of Tyler and Riley as her guys?

Pastor smiled. "They're not here yet, but I enjoyed meeting both of them at service this morning. Riley looked like a deer in the headlights, but it didn't take him long to get his bearings. I think after the fun we have tonight, he might feel better about being the new kid."

"He's been through a lot, Mike. He lost his dad several years ago, then recently his big brother in Iraq. His mother just moved to town to take a promotion, so he's trying to find how he fits into everything. It's been slow going at the ranch, but after he'd been a couple of times, I volunteered him to help with different riders."

Pastor Mike laughed. "Ah, that philosophy. 'I'm going to help you whether you want it or not.'"

Beth blushed. "Well, that's not *exactly* how it happened."

Pastor's brow arched.

A commotion at the door saved her from having to further put her foot in her mouth. She turned and saw Susan and Riley walking in. Tyler entered the building a moment later. A couple of the boys called out "hi." Riley nodded at them.

They checked in at the desk, and when Tyler looked up he saw Beth. They moved toward her.

"Hey, Riley," Beth greeted.

"You're back," Susan commented. "Riley was worried that you might not make it."

"I wouldn't have missed it even if I had to fix that fuel line myself."

Riley grinned.

Tyler stood behind Susan and studied Beth's outfit. "You're going in that?"

"I haven't had time to change since I flew in, but I will. I have to be ready to beat y'all at bowling and golf."

"You're going to try," Riley answered.

Beth slipped her arm around the boy. "You just watch and see."

"We'll see."

Pastor Mike stepped forward and shook Susan's and Riley's hands. "Good to see you, Susan, Riley. We're glad Riley came back for tonight's fun."

"I just wanted to drop off my son and make sure I didn't need to do something else."

"Not that I know of. We should be back at the church tomorrow morning around 7:00 a.m. We'll have breakfast for them if they are still up for eating and don't want to hit the sheets."

They all laughed.

Pastor shook Tyler's hand, then Riley's. "I think you're going to have a good time tonight." He faced Tyler. "I hope you're rested and ready for a full night. These kids are up to having a good time and want to blow all their energy for one final hurrah before school begins."

Beth wanted Pastor to quit talking. He was making it sound like they were going into battle.

"I've been in the Army, Pastor. I'm ready for this." Tyler's no-nonsense answer brought chuckles all around.

Despite the fun this night would be for the kids, Beth knew the work it entailed for the adults. The chaperones had to be on their toes, supervising and guiding the kids. Amazing, odd and indescribable things happen when you have close to a hundred teens together.

Pastor smiled. "I'm glad you're ready."

Riley held up his wrist. He had on what resembled a hospital ID. The yellow plastic bracelet had his name on it and a number and letter. "Why do I have this?"

Pastor Mike laughed. "Ask Beth here."

"Pastor," a voice called out.

He looked over their heads and excused himself.

All eyes turned back toward Beth, including the kids standing around Riley.

"Are you going to explain?" Tyler asked.

There was no way around it. "Well, my freshman year in high school, we went to the bowling alley and some of the guys were goofing off throwing water at each other. I accidentally stepped in between them and got hit with water from both sides. I went to the bathroom to dry off with one of those wall hand dryers. I didn't hear the call to get on the bus and the bus left without me. I called my mother and she came and got me and took me to the next event. After that lock-in, the church developed this system of tagging all the kids and assigning them to a team. Each adult is responsible for a group."

Riley grinned at Tyler as if sharing a good secret. Tyler barely contained his mirth.

Beth ignored them. "Another benefit of the system is the different places we go just look for the wristband to see who's with us. We don't want people joining who aren't part of the church group. It's for everyone's safety."

Several members of the youth group joined Riley and Tyler in their laughter.

After Riley finished laughing, he sobered. "That's a good idea."

Relief made her smile. "It makes the parents feel better about the night."

"I like that precaution," Susan added.

Riley looked around at the kids gathered in the

lobby of the multipurpose center. One of the boys Riley had met this morning came up and asked Riley if he'd like to hang with them. Riley accepted the invitation and moved off to another group of boys and girls.

Tyler studied Beth.

"What?"

He grinned. "You caused this labeling system?"

Resting her hands on her hips, she said, "Are you going to give me the same grief that my brothers did?"

"Yup."

Beth tried to be outraged, but the humor in his expression got to her. "Okay, it was my fault, but you need to realize we've never lost one of our teens on a lock-in."

"Only you."

"Watch out, Tyler, because if you don't, you just might get yours tonight."

"Are you threatening me?" From his tone, he wasn't worried.

"Nope, not me. I'm only stating facts."

"I can imagine your brothers' reactions." The sparkle in his brown eyes made her spirit soar. He had on a pair of jeans, boots and a blue shirt. The long sleeves were rolled up to his elbows.

She wanted to wrap her arm around his and invite him to talk to her. The man took her breath away. Over the past few weeks working on the ranch, in the heat of the summer, his skin had tanned and lighter streaks of brown ran though his hair.

"I need to get going," Susan said, bringing Beth out of her fantasy. "Would you two walk with me to my car?"

"Sure, and I can also grab my bag and change." She turned to Tyler, and he nodded.

Susan waited until they were by her white crossover vehicle before she said anything. Tears gathered in her eyes. "Thank you, both." She grasped Beth's hand and Tyler's. "After church this morning, Riley told me he was excited to come tonight. He even laughed at something one of the kids said to him." Moisture trickled down her cheeks. "That was the first time I'd heard my son laugh since Paul died."

Beth slipped her arms around the woman and hugged her. When she stepped back, Susan gave her a watery smile.

"Thank you."

"It's not me. If Tyler hadn't brought Riley— well, you should thank him."

"Tyler, you've been a godsend. Thank you for seeking us out when you came home." She brushed a kiss across Tyler's cheek.

Tyler appeared uncomfortable. Even guilty. "I just wanted to help any way I could."

"And so have you," Susan added, turning to Beth, squeezing her hand.

Beth returned the squeeze. "Riley touched my heart. In a way, he reminded me of my brother, who was in a dark place after he lost his leg. I guess I'm just too much of a busybody to walk away. At least, that's what my brothers say to me."

"Maybe God's using both of you to help my son. It's been so hard for him after Paul's death. After my husband died, I had to go to work. I got a job as a secretary and worked my way up. Paul was fourteen when my husband died. Riley six.

"Paul immediately got a job and contributed to the household. He also tried to be a dad for Riley. Paul even sent home most of his pay when he was in the Army. Riley was lost without Paul, more so than when his dad died. When I got an offer of a new job and a big promotion I thought the change of scenery would help us with a new beginning. I was afraid I'd never see my baby come back to me. Since Tyler's been here and Riley's been going to the ranch—"

The buses started up.

"We have to go." Beth brushed a kiss across Susan's cheek. "We'll take good care of him."

Susan nodded. Beth and Tyler raced back inside with a brief stop by Beth's car. Beth grabbed her bag and rushed into the bathroom to change. When she emerged, she had on jeans, a Second

Chance T-shirt and running shoes. After stashing her bag in the church office, she came back into the foyer.

Looking around, she saw Tyler leaning up against the wall, watching the milling crowds. A couple of girls saw each other and squealed in delight. Tyler pushed away from the wall, readying himself to react. When he saw the girls, he relaxed. Beth stepped to Tyler's side.

"Why'd they do that?" he muttered, nodding toward the squealing pair.

"Because they're girls."

He shook his head. The other teens around didn't even notice the hubbub. They kept talking.

Tyler looked as lost as her brothers in a Pink Pedals baby boutique, which they'd visited a couple of days ago because Sophie wanted to look at cribs. Zach hauled Ethan with him, claiming he wanted to share the experience.

"Weren't there any girls in your family?"

"No."

How thoughtless of her. But before she could apologize, he added, "But now that I think on it, my foster sister and her friends did a lot of squealing. I was drinking a Coke, when one of her girlfriends came over and told her some secret. The shrieking made me spill my Coke all over the counter. The least females should do is warn people they're going to do that."

Beth laughed at his disgruntled look. "It ain't going to happen, friend."

Pastor Mike got on the bullhorn and called the teens to attention. "Okay, guys. It's time to board the buses. On your tag, you've got a group number. The buses are labeled the same way. When you get out there, check in with the bus chaperone. First we're going to go miniature golfing. Afterward, we'll come back here for praise and worship, and pizza. Any questions?"

"What if someone falls asleep?" a boy in the back called out.

Pastor grinned. "The point, Ray, is to stay awake."

"What if he doesn't make it?" another person in the crowd asked.

"Well, last year, someone fell asleep and his hair got dyed green, so be warned."

The kids pointed at a teen. He raised his hands and said, "Okay, it was me, but I want to give that title to someone else. It took two weeks for it to wash out. Going to school the first day with green hair ain't cool."

Laughter filled the area. Several of the kids around him patted him on the back.

Tyler leaned down. "That happen in your day?"

"Yes."

"So what color was your hair the first day of school?"

Beth frowned at him, but inside she was overjoyed. She'd never seen Tyler so relaxed. He thought he'd gotten the upper hand when Beth had to admit that she was the reason for the tagging system. He was in for a big surprise.

As they boarded the bus, Beth caught Tyler looking at Riley and a pain appeared in his eyes. What was that about? She intended to find out.

Riley turned out to be an unbelievable golfer. He got two holes in one and beat Tyler by ten strokes. And Beth had golfing skills that blew Tyler away. Although she had only one hole in one, she beat him by seven strokes. They finished their second round and walked to the picnic tables. The concession stand located at the center of the three putt-putt courses and the video arcade was open, and the church had arranged for them to have drinks.

The night was beautiful, the breeze helped cool the heat of the day.

"You want something to drink?" Tyler asked Beth as they walked toward the concession stand.

"Water." She settled down on a picnic table under the patio awning. A fan attached to the awning circulated the air, cooling things down even more than the breeze.

Tyler picked up two bottles of water from the concession stand. From her perch sitting on the table top, she studied the kids finishing their rounds. Some of the boys found their way into the arcade.

Tyler handed her the bottle and joined her sitting on the table top. "You skunked me."

"You didn't ask if I played."

"And Riley beat us all."

Beth took a deep swallow from her bottle. "That was a surprise."

Tyler thought about it. "Paul told me he worked at a place like this when he was in high school. Riley spent a lot of time perfecting his game." The memory brought sorrow with it, but not the blinding pain it once would've. Beth grasped his hand and squeezed. That she saw and understood his pain awed him. She didn't probe but simply offered silent support, unlike what he'd had to deal with from his ex-fiancée.

Beth released his hand quickly, and he knew she didn't want the kids to see the adults holding hands. Beth had already broken up one young couple, warning them to keep their hands to themselves.

She took another swallow of water. "Riley certainly has his admirers, and that's what he needs." He was finishing his third round with a different set of teens who challenged him. He also had several female admirers.

Looking at Riley with the group, Tyler smiled. "He blew them away with his talent."

Riley made another hole-in-one on the last hole. The teens cheered, patting him on the back. They walked to the concession stand. Riley waved at them.

Beth waved back. "I think maybe that's what he needs, someone to admire his skill."

"Yeah." Tyler watched Riley. "It's amazing what a teenage girl's admiration can do for a teenage boy's self-image."

"Speaks a man of experience."

Looking down at her, he wanted to see if she was teasing, but her smile put his doubts to rest. "Okay, I remember a girl at church who was a friend of my foster sister, and she thought I was way cool because I played my guitar."

"You play?"

He shrugged. "It was the one thing I could take with me from foster home to foster home."

"That was you I heard the other day at the ranch?"

"Yes." He didn't want to talk anymore about his life. "So, how'd you get so good with your golf game?"

She didn't take her eyes off the kids as they moved to the video games arcade. Would she answer?

"The youth group's favorite pastime was playing miniature golf." She turned over the water bottle in her hand.

Tyler felt a pull to this woman. Nothing like the tempered emotions he'd felt when he was engaged. Of course, his heart and mind were still unsettled from the service this morning, and his talk with his foster family just added to his roiling emotions inside, so how could he make any sound judgment about anything? Too many changes bombarded him all at once, and he didn't know how to deal with it.

Riley laughed and the player of the game pounded the pinball machine.

"Let me try," Riley said. "I'm sure I can do better."

"I wish Susan could see her son now," Beth whispered.

One of the teen girls raced over to Beth and flopped down next to her.

"Why are guys such jerks?" she asked.

Tyler knew a minefield when he heard it. How was Beth going to navigate it?

"Well, that's kind of a broad question."

"Keith knows I wouldn't do what Jackie said I did."

Beth glanced over her shoulder. "Why don't we take a little walk and talk?"

The girl looked around Beth to Tyler. From the girl's expression, she thought all men were lower life forms. "Okay." They walked away.

"You don't mind, do you?" Beth asked over her shoulder.

Tyler didn't take offense. "No, go ahead, please." Later he could ask how she fared, but honestly, he didn't want to be involved in the teenage girl's drama, nor was he qualified. His foster sister wasn't into drama, but she had friends who came to the house to cry and pout. His foster brothers left the house when that kind of thing happened. Even his foster father left. It only took Tyler one time to understand the wisdom of that route.

The memories brought peace. He hadn't thought of those times in a long time. The Olaskys had given him rules, structure, but also an abundance of love. And they'd changed his life by taking him to church.

A cheer went up from the boys. Tyler stood and walked to the pinball machine. The boy who'd just finished danced with victory.

"Hey, Tyler, can you outdo Mick's score?"

Several of the other guys urged him to try. Riley nodded for him to play.

"It's not fair for the adults to compete," he explained, trying to get out of it. It had the opposite effect. Looking around, he knew his words challenged every male.

"You chicken?" one boy asked. Several other boys echoed that sentiment.

Riley stepped forward to hear the answer.

"All right, I'll take you up on the challenge, but I don't want any crying foul at the end of the game."

He looked around and each teen agreed to the terms. Tyler stepped up to the pinball machine, pulled back the plunger, sending the first ball into motion.

The teens gathered around to watch. Tyler's spirit felt lighter than it had in years. When was the last time he'd had fun?

Chapter Nine

❧

They went back to the church for the praise service and a short sermon from one of the teens. After the worship, they moved to the fellowship hall and dove into a dozen pizzas that were waiting. There was also a salad bowl next to the boxes of pizza, bread sticks and dessert pizza covered in cinnamon and sugar.

Riley piled his paper plate with four different pieces of pizza, bread sticks and dessert, but avoided the salad.

Beth grabbed a paper plate. "Are you enjoying yourself?"

Riley took several packets of Parmesan cheese. "It's been great. Did you see Tyler with that pinball machine earlier?"

"No, but I heard the roar when I was with the girls." She had spied Tyler at the pinball machine with a crowd gathered around him.

"He blew the top out of the game. He got the highest number recorded and made all the guys shake their heads. One guy tried to beat him, but none could. You know, some of them asked Tyler and me about if they could come to see the ranch?" Riley's chest puffed out.

"What did you tell them?"

"I said I thought it would be fine. Tyler agreed and said he'd check with you and Zach."

"We could always use more volunteers." Tyler's tact with the kids impressed Beth. "Did you tell them about what we do?"

"I kinda added to what Tyler said." He grabbed a plastic cup filled with Coke. "The guys are wowed with Tyler being a soldier."

"And are the girls impressed with your work at the ranch?"

He shrugged, but his neck turned red. He went back to his table.

Beth wondered if it was Riley that volunteered that information about the ranch or if it was Tyler. She put a piece of pineapple and Canadian bacon pizza on her plate. As she added salad, she noticed the group of boys talking to Tyler. It appeared he had a fan club. Well, her plan certainly had worked well.

"Your friends have won over the kids," Pastor Mike commented, picking up a paper plate.

"It's a blessing to see Riley smiling. You should've seen him when he first showed up at Second Chance. The chip on his shoulder was so big, I'm surprised he could walk." Tyler hadn't been much better. "I prayed for Riley, and I think my prayers have been answered."

"Well, he certainly is connecting with the other kids." Pastor helped himself to several pieces of pizza and salad. "I'm glad Riley's enjoying himself, and hope he'll start coming on a regular basis." He grabbed a drink and went to sit with the teens.

Beth settled next to one of the other chaperones and a friend from high school, Kelly Upton. Kelly had grown up in the church and was in the graduating class before Beth.

"Well, I will say that you've certainly caused a stir among all the girls and guys," Kelly said.

"What are you talking about?" Beth dug into her salad.

"The hunk."

"Okay, you're going to have to be more specific." But Beth knew who Kelly was talking about.

"The tall guy with brooding eyes." She pointed with her piece of pizza at Tyler. "I saw him this morning at service and had all sorts of ideas. But when he showed up tonight and attached himself to you, well, I knew he was taken."

Beth choked on her salad.

Kelly patted her on the back. Beth grabbed her plastic cup and took a drink.

"So who is he?" Kelly pressed.

Beth studied the aforementioned male. She couldn't fault Kelly for her attraction to Tyler. But oddly enough she didn't want to share with Kelly.

"So, you've laid claim to him."

If Kelly had kicked her under the table, Beth couldn't have been more surprised. "What are you talking about?"

Kelly put down her piece of pizza and covered Beth's hand with hers. "It's been a long time since high school, Beth."

The bottom fell out for Beth. Kelly had been the one person who had witnessed the incident with Gavin. Gavin and Beth had been the golden couple of their senior class. Gavin, the handsome, tall quarterback, with a dazzling smile and quick wit, had snagged Beth, the girl voted most liked in her junior yearbook.

Gavin transferred in the last weeks of their junior year. When he'd asked her to the homecoming game and dance their senior year, Beth had been in heaven and the envy of every girl in school. Gavin's charm offensive had so overwhelmed Beth that she fell head over heels in love with him. At first, she didn't notice his subtle manipulation of her. They hung out with his friends, went where he wanted and did what he wanted. He came with her to church a few times and dazzled her friends, parents and most adults.

It had taken months for Beth to wake up. Her normally bubbly outlook disappeared. She felt stupid. After she'd talked to a friend—a boy she'd known since second grade—at one school basketball game, Gavin told her he didn't want her to associate with him anymore. He wasn't good enough for her.

That incident woke her up. That had been in early March. Beth spent the rest of that month and April trying to figure out how to end the relationship without people knowing why.

They'd gone to the senior prom together. Afterward, they went out for ice cream at the local drive-in with several other couples. Kelly had been there, back from college. Beth wanted to know how the year had gone. When Gavin told her they were leaving, Beth told him she wasn't finished talking to Kelly. He slapped her across the face for sassing him.

Kelly had stood up to the football hero and asked if Beth wanted to ride home with her. Beth knew if Kelly took her home, the wrath of her brothers and dad would rain down upon Gavin. She told Kelly she was okay.

When Gavin took her home, he told her he wouldn't have done that if she hadn't acted so badly. The boy never got near her again. Kelly had called the next morning, making sure she was all right. Beth told her she was done with Gavin and asked Kelly not to say anything to anyone.

Kelly kept her end of the bargain. Luckily, they'd been done with classes and Beth didn't have to be around Gavin again.

Beth never told her parents what had happened. They questioned her about why she hadn't seen Gavin off when he left for a summer vacation in Europe with his family. She never gave them a satisfactory answer. She saw the questions in their eyes, but they didn't press her.

After that incident, Beth's heart closed down. It took the summer for her to recover her normally bright outlook on life. She eventually became comfortable around men. She even dated a couple of times, but broke things off before they got serious.

"It's about time," Kelly said, bringing Beth around from her brooding.

A frown gathered on Beth's brow. "What are you talking about?"

"You. You've acted like men are toxic for a long time."

Beth opened her mouth to protest, but Kelly held up her hand.

"You had reason, friend. I understand that. Later, I heard from others they noticed how con-

trolling Gavin could be. Even so, they were mes-
merized by his charm."

"You didn't say—"

"I didn't say anything, so don't worry. Only you
and I know. But when you visited church while
you were at UNM and afterward, I watched you
blow off a lot of nice guys. I heard someone say,
if you want advice, talk to Beth. But if you want
a date, don't waste your breath. I'm glad you're
finally willing to step on out there."

Beth gaped at her friend.

"It's time."

Beth glanced at Tyler. He finished grabbing
several pieces of pizza and a drink. He walked
toward them.

Kelly elbowed Beth. "And when you decided to
dive back in, you did a good job."

Tyler placed his plate across from Beth and sat.
He nodded toward Kelly. "Tyler Lynch."

Kelly smiled back. "Kelly Upton."

"Nice to meet you." He took a bite of his pizza.

Kelly bumped Beth with her elbow. "I haven't
seen you around here before."

"Beth volunteered me to chaperone tonight's
events."

"She did?"

"He works for Zach and Sophie, helping with
the horses and around the ranch," Beth explained.

"So you're a ranch hand?" Kelly pressed.

Beth felt Kelly's amusement and she wanted to squirm.

"I grew up on a farm, but I ran into Zach in Albuquerque and he offered me a job."

"Out of the blue?"

"No, Kelly," Beth answered. "Zach and Tyler were in the Army together, and we needed more help with all the veterans we are getting. You should come by sometime and see what we're doing. Your company might want to become a corporate sponsor of the ranch. It's good PR." Beth motioned to the logo on her T-shirt.

"That's an idea. I'll run it by my boss." Kelly turned to Tyler and gave him a toothy smile. "So, Tyler, tell me about yourself."

He shrugged. "There's nothing much to tell."

"Surely not."

Beth didn't pay attention to the rest of the conversation, her mind too caught up in what Kelly had said. Was what Kelly said true? Had she emotionally hidden herself away, not allowing anyone close? Surely not. Kelly had got it wrong.

Beth glanced at Tyler's face. His closed-off demeanor was no longer there, and he was talking with Kelly, actually engaging in conversation.

What had happened to that reticent man who had come to Second Chance several months ago? When had he changed?

Maybe that's why she'd been so attracted to him

from the first, they were similar souls who'd been hurt. Or was it because she felt Tyler was safe? If he wasn't willing to open up, then she wouldn't have to worry about him getting too close.

She shoved away the thought. Now wasn't the time to wrestle with this nonsense. She was here to chaperone teenagers, not to dwell on her love-lorn status.

Period.

End of story.

Too bad her heart didn't buy the argument.

Tyler watched the boys race back and forth in the gym, shooting baskets. The girls were scattered throughout the room. Riley grabbed the basketball and dribbled it. Another boy grabbed the ball away from him. Riley snatched it back and shot the hoop. He made it.

"Way to go, Riley." Tyler whooped and clapped. Riley shot him a grin. Susan would be jumping for joy. Tyler knew he was keeping his promise to Paul. His heart eased.

Pastor Mike entered the room and announced the buses would leave in ten minutes for Castle Rock Super Center. "Finish up your game, make pit stops. You need to be outside and ready to go. We've got bowling, wall climbing, bumper cars and more video games." He walked out of the gym.

The stampede nearly flattened Tyler. After the

girls filed into the bathroom, Tyler walked back down the hall, passing the smaller sanctuary. The lead singer on the worship team sat with his guitar.

Tyler paused at the door. "You've got talent."

"Thanks. You play?"

"I do. It was the best chick magnet in high school."

The teen laughed. "Yeah, still is. You any good?"

Tyler shrugged. "It's been a while since I seriously played."

The teen held up his guitar. "Give it a shot."

Suddenly there was a longing in Tyler's soul he couldn't ignore. He walked down the center aisle, took the guitar and sat on the top step. His fingers began to strum the notes of the worship song they played at services in Iraq.

Kelly and Beth finished cleaning up the fellowship room after consolidating all the remaining pieces of pizza into one box. "You never know who might want a piece with breakfast." Kelly grinned.

"That's gross."

"I ate my share in college. But I had coffee with t."

Beth shook her head. "I think I'd skip the pizza or breakfast."

Kelly stopped and looked around the room.

"You know, in this day and age of enlightenment, guys should be in here helping us clean up."

"You don't see any girls in here, either. As a matter of fact, there's not a teen in sight."

"We did this wrong."

"When we do a review of tonight, bring up that point."

As they walked down the hall to the main entrance, the sound of a guitar and a wonderful baritone voice filled the air.

"Who's that?" Kelly asked. "He's good."

Beth and Kelly stopped by the open sanctuary doors.

Tyler sat on one of the steps to the stage, guitar in hand, singing the latest worship chorus by a popular Christian artist.

Beth stepped into the room and joined in on the chorus.

Kelly had joined Beth in singing the chorus. When Tyler paused, Beth said, "Don't stop."

The kids at the doorway filed into the room. "Let's finish it," one of the boys said. He ran to the stage and jumped on it and picked up his guitar. Two other teens joined them on the stage and began to play the balance of the song. The lead singer sat at the keyboard.

Tyler smiled at Beth and started singing the rest of the praise chorus. By the time they sang the last line of the chorus, every teen, chaperone and the pastor stood in the sanctuary, joining in the praise.

When the last note died down, a silence settled on the group. Finally, one of the teens standing in the aisle said, "That was great. Maybe we should get together at eleven every Sunday night and do a little singing."

The atmosphere instantly changed, and several of the kids laughed.

"On the buses, guys," Pastor Mike announced.

Several of the teens gave Tyler a high five as they boarded the bus. Tyler settled in the seat next to Riley. Beth took the seat across from them.

"You're good," Riley commented to Tyler, a note of pride in Riley's voice. "I think you won over some of the guys."

"I'm glad." Tyler didn't know why he'd picked up the guitar, but there had been a need in his soul. Last week, he'd picked up his guitar for the first time in months and tried some choruses. That's when Beth caught him.

Things were shifting inside him at lightning speed. Was he ready for that?

"How'd you know the words to that song?" Riley asked.

Beth leaned forward. "I was wondering the same thing."

He tried to remain casual. "That was one of the new worship songs our chaplain used in services."

Riley looked at Beth. "Wasn't he good?"

"He was, and he can sing. We're learning all sorts of things about him tonight."

Not comfortable with the direction of this conversation, Tyler said, "Same for me. I now know not to challenge Riley or Beth to any games of miniature golf."

Riley grinned. "How are you in math? I'm going to need some help with algebra this year."

"I was better in shop." Tyler turned to Beth. "You any good in math?"

Beth gave them a thumbs-up. "I've got you covered."

Tyler bumped Riley with his elbow. "See, you've got help coming out your ears."

The sounds of bowling pins being knocked down rang through the bowling alley part of the Castle Rock Super Center. Riley cheered Tyler's strike. Castle Rock was a massive complex that housed a fifty-lane bowling alley, a huge video arcade, a room of bumper cars and a room filled with four climbing walls.

"Wow, that's so cool. All those pins just rise up together and fall." Riley stood up from his seat and gave Tyler a five-knuckled tap.

Beth marked the strike. In the sixth frame, Tyler's score was 94 through the fifth frame with his strike requiring one more roll to score it. He wasn't doing too badly but the Army always had bowling alleys somewhere on base. Of course, in Iraq, the soldiers made their own bowling pins with empty water bottles and a small ball.

"You're making all the kids drool," Beth told him.

Tyler sat in the chair next to her. She wasn't too bad herself with a score of 80. She hadn't bowled this frame and had a spare last frame. He leaned over to look more closely at the overhead score sheet. Riley had 70, Sam 71 and Grace 66. "What are you talking about?"

She raised her brow. "You might want to let one of them beat you."

"Seriously?"

She looked at Riley throw his ball down the alley.

Tyler leaned close, smelling the scent of orange blossoms on Beth, momentarily distracting him. He swallowed. "If I started throwing gutter balls now, the kids would know what I was doing. Besides, remember I told you you always play to your strongest card."

She turned her head and his lips were inches from hers. All he could think to do was move two inches forward. The kids yelling broke into the moment.

Riley's ball crossed the head pin and struck between the first and second pins. All the pins went down except the seven. It wobbled.

"C'mon and fall," Beth called out, jumping up as if her actions could change the tide.

Shouts from his teammates urged the pin to fall, too. It wobbled and rocked, but hung on and didn't fall down.

"Aaah," came the collective sound.

"You can make that spare, Riley," Beth called out, giving him a thumbs-up.

Riley picked up his ball and went for the spare.

Her encouragement of Riley warmed Tyler's heart. This was a kid she didn't know a month ago, and yet, Beth wouldn't let him slip through the cracks back then or now. Her empathy and encouraging manner made him spill his guts when he hadn't volunteered information to anyone else. What was it about this woman?

Standing, Beth danced to the left side as if her action could influence the ball as it rolled toward the pin. At the last minute, the ball fell into the gutter.

Riley's shoulders slumped.

"It's okay, Riley. I didn't get my first spare,

either." Beth patted him on the back, then grabbed, aimed and launched her ball. Her form was good.

"She's nice," Riley commented, taking Beth's seat.

Tyler's head whipped around. Riley continued to look at Beth. Slowly, Riley smiled.

"She likes you."

Tyler nearly choked.

Beth went after her 6-10 split. She picked off the 10.

"Sorry, Beth," Riley yelled out. He gave Beth his seat and went to sit beside Grace. Beth settled in the chair and scored her frame.

Tyler's mind still grappled with Riley's comment. Was he giving off some vibe that told the world he was attracted to Beth? Was he? Was Beth getting those vibes, too?

He knew the answer to that question, but he didn't feel worthy of that love. When the stakes were high, he failed those he loved.

"What's wrong?" Beth's question let him know that his poker-face failed.

"Do you have a boyfriend?" The question popped out of his mouth, shocking him as much as Beth. Where had that come from? He scrambled. "Uh, what I meant was, am I going to have a visit from an irate male, wondering why you're spending so much time at Second Chance?" His second explanation wasn't any better than his explosive question.

Beth watched Grace bowl.

What's wrong with you, Lynch? he chastised himself. Of course, no one had ever accused him of being a silver-tongued devil who could talk his way out of any situation. He usually just kept his trap shut and that worked well. But in this situation, it wasn't going to work. "I'm sorry, Beth. It's none of my business."

After she wrote the bowler's score, she glanced at him. "True."

She wasn't going to make this easy.

Looking down at the score sheet, her mouth pulled up into a smile. "Currently, I am unattached."

The awkwardness of his words lifted and Beth's smile righted the world. Breathing a huge sigh of relief, he relaxed. After the rush of stupidity evaporated, he wondered why she wasn't already married or at least had a steady boyfriend. She was a beautiful woman with a bubbling personality who seemed never to know a stranger. Or accept a bad attitude. His hand covered hers this time, and he squeezed. She glanced shyly at him and smiled.

Behind them, someone cleared their throat. Beth slipped her hand out from under his. Pastor Mike leaned over their shoulders as if to look at the scores.

"I'm glad to see everyone bowling so well. Have you had any problems with the kids fraternizing?"

Beth's cheeks turned beet red. "None I couldn't handle."

Mike rested his hands on Beth's and Tyler's shoulders, looking at each of them. "That's good. Let's set a good example for the kids."

"Okay," she mumbled.

Mike nailed Tyler with a look of warning. Tyler nodded his understanding.

With a final pat, Pastor Mike, straightened. "When y'all finish your game, most of the kids are gravitating to the video game room."

They nodded.

Neither said anything for several moments. Beth squirmed in the pregnant silence. Finally, Beth mumbled, "Your turn."

He got up and bowled a strike.

"You're hot," Riley yelled.

The innocent statement hit Tyler right between the eyes. He stared at Riley, purposely avoiding looking at Beth. "I'm on a roll, for sure." He picked up his ball and threw a strike. Why couldn't it have been a spare, then he would've had enough time to get his scattered thoughts together.

When he sat beside her, she whispered, "You're on a roll for sure."

He didn't dare look at her, because if he did, he might reveal more than he was ready to.

Chapter Ten

After they finished their round of bowling, Beth, Riley and Grace decided to try the climbing walls. Tyler started to go with them, but several boys challenged Tyler to a video game.

Tyler looked at Beth.

"Go ahead. We'll be in the rock climbing arena."

Riley grinned. "Go ahead, Tyler. I think there are several guys who want to play you."

The competitive looks in the kids' faces got to Tyler.

"I'll see you guys later." Tyler walked into the video arcade with several boys.

Beth felt proud of Tyler. He set a strong example for the kids, especially Riley. He went up in her admiration.

Beth, Riley and Grace walked down the hall, past the bumper cars to the climbing arena.

Beth looked around the room. Two walls had

been fashioned for climbing, with footholds on the artificial rock wall. In the center of the room were harnesses attached to the ceiling. After several minutes of watching others climb and having the kids call out to them, Riley encouraged Grace to climb the wall first. She tried. Riley, along with the worker assigned to the room, held the rope for Grace as she climbed. She only made it up halfway before she slipped and Riley had to stabilize her. Grace squealed. Beth talked to Grace while Riley and the worker lowered her to the ground.

Grace laughed when her feet touched the ground. Slipping out of the harness, she encouraged Riley. "You try."

Riley took up the challenge. Turning to Beth, he said, "Want to race?"

Beth wasn't sure how she'd do, but seeing Riley come to life gave her reason enough to accept the challenge. Besides, she couldn't resist a dare. "But who will spot me?"

Pastor Mike, who had just walked into the room, volunteered to spot for Beth.

Beth and Riley moved to the climbing wall. They were halfway up the wall when Tyler walked in the room. Grace and the worker held Riley's line.

Another teen wanted to climb and Tyler volunteered to take the worker's place. Tyler placed his hands above the worker's and took control of the rope. Grace's hands had turned white from her grip.

"I've got it," Tyler whispered to her.

Grace nodded and released the rope, but didn't leave. She continued to stare up at Riley, smiling.

"Go, Riley. You're in the lead," Grace called out.

Riley looked at Beth. She was a couple of footholds below him.

"Are you still the champ?" Pastor quietly asked Tyler.

"They didn't have an old-fashioned pinball machine. Only video games, and Manny beat me."

"You sound relieved."

Tyler's gaze never left Riley. "It's good for Manny. Bragging rights as a teenage boy are important."

"Good observation."

Tyler shrugged.

"I won," Riley shouted, touching the top.

"Yeah," Grace shouted, clapping.

"Only by a hair," Beth replied, reaching the top of the wall.

They looked down and Riley's grin warmed Tyler's heart. The two at the top rappelled down. Once they were on the ground, Beth and Riley urged Tyler to try the wall. He refused. "I did all my climbing in the service. I'm not in any shape to do it now."

"You chicken?" Riley challenged.

Tyler knew Pastor and Beth watched him. "Let's just say, I know the limits of my body now. I'm sure Prince Charming won't be happy if I end up hurting myself and then someone else would have to feed him. I'm going to be cautious."

"Beth went."

She didn't say anything, waiting.

"Well, she's younger and weighs a whole lot less than me."

Riley thought about it. "True."

Leaning down, Tyler whispered, "You think you can convince him to give it up?"

"Maybe we should let him off the hook," Beth said. "It could be embarrassing if you beat him again."

"But he won at bowling," Riley countered.

"Yeah, but as he said his body's older than yours and it wears out quicker."

Understanding lit Riley's eyes. He patted Tyler on the arm. "It's okay. I understand."

Tyler didn't know whether or not to be insulted.

"C'mon, let's try the bumper cars, Grace."

She nodded and they walked out of the room.

Tyler still held Beth. Pastor Mike looked at Tyler.

"You've won the argument. You can put Beth down."

Immediately, Tyler's left arm relaxed and Beth's

feet swung down. Tyler had to squat a little for her to touch the floor. When her feet touched, he completely released her.

Beth refused to look at him.

"I'm going to try bumper cars, too." She darted out of the room.

Tyler looked at Pastor Mike. "Sorry."

Pastor Mike laughed and patted Tyler on the shoulder. "Just make sure it doesn't happen again."

At 3:45 a.m., all the teens were going strong, but that could be due to the continuous supply of soft drinks they'd gulped down. They moved from the bumper cars to another wing that housed the video games.

The teens might be going strong, but Tyler felt each of his thirty-five years, because he wanted to close his eyes and take a power nap, much like he did in Iraq. The bumper cars had been fun and a mental release, driving around and slamming into others. He thought the Army should have that as a debriefing when soldiers came home to use up the extra energy you needed in a war zone.

Beth gravitated to the ping-pong tables with three other teens while Riley moved to a video game.

Since Beth had drafted him as a chaperone, Tyler had worried he might not be about to handle being around teens for a continuous twelve hours.

Only within the past few weeks—since he'd been at the ranch—had he finally felt comfortable and easy around people. He'd also realized the hyper vigilance that a war zone requires of a soldier had begun to retreat. The knot in his gut had eased.

His fears about tonight evaporated. In fact, he'd enjoyed the night for more than one reason.

Riley grabbed two cans of Coke and walked to where Tyler sat. "Want one?" He held up the can.

"What I really need is a cup of coffee, but this is welcome." He accepted the can.

Riley sat on the bench next to Tyler. The boy took a long drink. After several moments of silence, Tyler said, "You look like you're enjoying yourself."

"I'm having a blast."

"You need to thank Beth. She's the one who suggested this to me."

"She's somethin', isn't she?" Riley glanced at Beth.

Tyler knew a loaded question when he heard it. "Yes, she is."

"When she made me help with the horses, I thought she was a nutcase. And bossy."

Tyler didn't laugh out loud, but grinned. "I'd say so. She was kinda that way with Dogger."

Riley's eyes went wide. "Really?"

"I'm not sure how she worked it, but one day I

walked into the stables and there she was petting him. And he was eating it up."

"I understand." He nodded his head and took another swig of his drink.

"So you like her, too, don't you?"

Why was everyone singing this same song? "Sure I like her. And I like working at the ranch, too."

Riley choked on his drink.

So even this teenager wasn't buying his denial.

"Well, if you want my opinion, I think she likes you back."

This time it was Tyler who nearly choked. "Why do you say that?"

Riley leaned close and whispered, "'Cause Pastor Mike had to break up the handholding between you two."

Wanting to crawl under the table, Tyler scrambled for an answer.

Riley patiently waited.

A little guidance, here, Lord, would be appreciated. Immediately Tyler knew what to do. When he was Riley's age, he wanted honesty. "That was kind of embarrassing, wasn't it?"

He nodded. "You didn't answer my question."

Tyler couldn't help appreciating Riley's persistence. It was good to see him so engaged. "Yeah, I like Beth."

"I knew it."

He'd been made. "But it's been a while since I've had a girlfriend, so I'm going to take it slow. I'm feeling a little rusty."

Riley nodded as if he knew exactly what Tyler was talking about. Riley fell silent, staring at his can. Slowly he looked at Tyler.

"What is it?" Tyler asked. "You can ask me anything. Now if it's about the birds and bees, I might stutter."

Riley remained quiet for a moment, then asked, "Did you want to be my friend because of my brother?"

The kid threw him a curve. Tyler wasn't expecting *that* question. "What do you mean?"

"Are you being nice to me because you promised my brother to be my friend?" Riley looked down again.

Tyler fought the panic. He needed to be careful with his answer. "Paul and I were good friends. We both lost our dads early."

That grabbed Riley's attention. "Really?"

"Really. I was eight when the tornado ripped though our house in Oklahoma. Both of my parents were killed."

"Oh. Do you have brothers or sisters?"

"No, it was just me. So your brother and I had a lot of things in common. Paul was good with ordnance—bombs—and so am I. Paul could disarm any bomb."

"He was good at fixin' things. If something broke around the house, he'd fix it or find a way to get it fixed. I remember when the TV broke he worked out a deal with the TV repairman, cleaning his shop for six weeks. My mom worked long hours, so most the time it was just Paul and me.

"But when he started working for Funland, things got better. Not only did I get to play miniature golf, I got to eat lots of Frito pies and hog dogs."

"Paul told me a lot about you—really, it was bragging."

"Yeah?"

"Yeah. When I saw you playing golf earlier, I remembered him talking about how good you were. We traded stories about our high school jobs. I worked at delivering electronics for a place in Tulsa." He laughed. "We traded stupid stories."

"What's that?"

"Our mess-ups."

"Like when Paul put too much popcorn in the machine at the concession stand, and he brought home bags and bags of popcorn?"

"Yes, like that one. I also heard about you getting stuck in the windmill hole, goofing off. It took nearly an hour to get you out. He had to call the firemen to rescue you."

Riley laughed. "I wanted to see what was inside the little house. So what was your stupid story?"

Tyler rubbed his chin. "Well, I was delivering a big TV. The people had a sunken living room and I didn't know it and I tripped. I was the guy walking backward. The TV landed on the edge of the coffee table, breaking the TV and the table."

"What happened?"

"Since everything was busted, we had to bring out a new TV, and I ended up paying for the coffee table."

"Wow, that's bad."

"I was nervous, but my foster father talked the store out of firing me." That was a critical point where Tyler knew he could trust his foster parents. The mercy and understanding they gave him undercut his bitterness. So why had he decided they wouldn't understand him after he came back from Iraq?

Riley's hand ran over the can. "I really don't remember too much of my dad, but Paul understood when I messed up."

"I heard a couple of stories."

"Really."

"Something about the next door neighbors' tree and several branches," Tyler whispered. "Paul also had pictures of you guys. And I know he loved the emails he got from you."

"That was the best time of the day, when I got home from school and opened my email. Paul's would be there. I miss it."

"Do you know that Dogger was Paul's best friend, too? Dogger liked everyone in our unit, but it was Paul and me that Dogger would settle down with when we sacked out."

They sat quietly beside each other.

"Hey, Riley, are you going to try to beat me?" Beth called out.

"You sure you can handle it?" Riley called back.

"Bring it on."

Riley stood. "Thanks, Tyler. I wondered why you came to the house and were nice to me."

"I wanted to tell your mother what a good man Paul was, and I was sorry he died."

Riley nodded and moved to the ping-pong table. As Tyler watched the match between Beth and Riley, hope swelled in his heart. If he couldn't save Paul, he might be able to help Riley. Paul would like that.

At five-fifteen in the morning, they boarded the bus for the final trip back to the church. Beth checked over her clipboard, making sure she had everyone on her list.

The kids on the bus teased Sam Boyett. He was found asleep in the bowling alley. He woke up when the kids were trying to dye his hair green. They only got half of his head dyed.

Beth stood at the front of the bus by the driver. "Listen up, guys. When we get back to church, breakfast will be in the fellowship hall. Parents should be arriving shortly after that to pick you up. Don't leave until you check out with Kelly, Tyler or me. You don't want me showing up at your house, checking your bedroom to make sure you are there. Understand?"

Laughter answered her question.

"I need to hear you," Beth pressed.

"Yes," came the reply in unison.

Beth made her way to the back of the bus to sit beside Tyler.

"How you holding up?" she asked.

"I'm too old for this. I'll probably go home and fall face-first into the mattress."

"Me, too, except maybe not face-first." She pulled out her chapstick from her jeans and ran it over her lips. "You think Dogger's worried that you left him?"

"No. My things are still at the house. He's not worried." He knew his dog.

Resting her head against the seat back, her eyes fluttered closed. Instantly, she was asleep.

Tyler's heart skipped a beat.

"Should we dye her hair?" Kelly whispered, nodding at Beth. Kelly sat across the aisle from them. "Or just let it slip?"

Tyler smiled down at the sleeping woman. "I think we can let it slip. She drove the teens through the night, so I think she deserves some slack."

Kelly studied Beth. After several moments, her eyes moved to Tyler. "I hope you're as good as Beth thinks."

His mouth opened to protest, but Kelly shook her head. "She's a woman with an amazing heart. I've seen her give and give to others, helping when others give up. She deserves someone who cares for her."

"You're misreading things."

Sitting back, Kelly studied them. "I'm not the one who's misreading things. She's been hurt badly before."

Tyler's mind flew to the man he'd seen on Friday talking to Beth at the store where she worked. It had been obvious to him that there was a history between the two. He'd instantly disliked the man. There'd been a swagger, an arrogance about him. It had been obvious to Tyler that Beth hadn't wanted to have anything to do with him. Had that been the guy who hurt her?

Beth stirred, shifting and settling her head against Tyler's arm. When he looked up to deny what Kelly had said, she'd moved to the front of the bus.

What had happened to Beth?

When he compared Beth with his ex-fiancée, the difference was night and day. His ex was needy, whiney and worried about what others thought. Beth, on the other hand, was a force of nature, bringing others along in her wake, but she always took people to a place that would help them.

Her weight on his arm felt right, but the bus turned the corner and pulled into the church parking lot. He gently shook Beth awake. "Beth, Beth," he whispered. "We're here."

Her eyelids fluttered open and those big green eyes slowly focused.

"You better snap to, girl, or the kids will know that you've been asleep."

That was all it took. She bolted upright. Her gaze moved around to make sure no one had caught her. She finally looked at him.

"I'll keep your secret. And you don't have green hair."

She smiled back. "Thanks." She brushed a kiss across his cheek.

Standing, she headed for the front of the bus. "We're here, guys. Remember, breakfast's in the fellowship hall and check with Kelly, Tyler or me before you leave with your parents."

Beth marked off another teen on her list. Three teens were left, Riley, Grace and Wendy. Wendy had just said goodbye to her girlfriends.

"I had fun with you, Riley," Grace whispered to Riley. They sat on the floor waiting for parents to pick them up.

He grinned. "I did, too."

"I hope you'll come to church again." Shyly, she looked down at her hands.

"I will."

"He's a goner," Tyler whispered in Beth's ear.

Beth jerked in surprise. The man had a way of sneaking up on her. "I think you're right."

Grace's mother rushed in the building. "I'm sorry I'm late. There was a bad wreck on Singing Arrow. There were several police cars, fire engines and the ambulance. It had traffic backed up for several miles."

The street that Grace's mother referred to was the major four-lane street close to the church. "I think I saw Wendy's parents' van caught in the mess."

Grace and Riley smiled at each other and she left with her mother. Several minutes later, Wendy's dad arrived, confirming what they'd learned earlier.

"It was a mess," the man said, shaking his head. "One car was torn in half. They were loading the ambulance with one of the victims. The firemen were still working on getting the person out of the other vehicle. I prayed for the folks in the wreck."

The man wrapped his arms around his daughter. "Did you have a good time?" They disappeared out the glass doors leading to the parking lot.

After another twenty minutes, Beth knew something was wrong. She pulled Tyler aside. "Have you called Susan?"

"Yeah, and there's no answer." He looked at Riley, who'd fallen asleep sitting on the floor, his back against the wall. "Something's wrong."

"Try her number one more time."

He walked into the church office to use the phone. Pastor Mike was in the church office, taking care of the bill for the charter company. Tyler dialed Susan one more time. The line was picked up.

"Who's speaking?" The tone of Tyler's voice warned Beth something wasn't right. His expression hardened, making her heart sink.

"I understand. No. No one, but her teenage son. What hospital?" He listened. "We'll be there." He hung up. "That wreck Grace's mother talked about, that was Susan's car."

Beth's stomach plunged.

Pastor Mike walked out of the office. "What's happening?"

Tyler explained.

"So how is Susan?" Beth asked.

"I don't know, but the cop wanted to know about her family. He wants us to go to the hospital."

Riley appeared in the doorway, rubbing the sleep from his eyes. "Hey, you deserted me. I'm lucky the other kids weren't here. Where's mom?"

Beth blanched and swallowed hard.

"What's wrong?" Riley demanded, his voice unsteady, looking at each adult.

"Your mom's been in an accident," Tyler explained.

"What? What happened? How bad was it?"

Beth stepped to his side and put her arm around Riley's shoulders. "We don't know. All we know is what hospital she's been taken to."

Fear clouded Riley's eyes. "Not mom, too."

Beth pulled his face to her shoulder and looked at Tyler. Pain radiated off of him.

"We need to go."

Chapter Eleven

Beth and Riley climbed into Tyler's truck and drove to the hospital. The University of New Mexico Hospital had the only Level One trauma center in the city.

Riley sat shell-shocked in the front seat of the truck between Beth and Tyler. Beth laid her hand on his. He didn't pull away. After a few moments, he unclenched his fist and turned his palm up and wrapped his fingers around Beth's in a death grip.

Out of the corner of his eye, Tyler saw Beth's effort. He knew exactly what pain Riley felt. He was younger when he lost both of his parents, but the pain didn't lessen no matter what the age.

Beth directed Tyler to the hospital.

When they arrived at the emergency room, it was almost empty. Beth checked in with the receptionist, explaining who they were. A moment later, a cop came out of the double doors leading to the trauma area. The desk attendant directed him to Riley, Beth and Tyler.

"I'm Sergeant Raul Meraz. Are you related to Susan Carter?"

"I am," Riley said. "I'm her son."

The cop frowned. "How old are you?"

"Thirteen."

Tyler stepped in. "Sergeant, I'm the one you spoke to earlier. Riley is Susan's only living relative. We are good friends of Susan's and Riley was with us for a church event."

"An all-night lock-in with the youth group," Beth added. "Can you tell us what's happening?"

He thought about it for a moment. "From the witnesses at the scene, Ms. Carter was traveling east on the street. A truck on one of the side streets ran the stop sign and broadsided Ms. Carter's truck. A third car hit the back of Ms. Carter's car, knocking her into another car in the far left lane."

"No," Riley cried, doubling over in pain. He raced out the double doors.

"I'll go to him," Beth whispered. "Tyler, you get the details." The glass doors opened with a whoosh.

"How is she doing?" Tyler asked the policeman.

"They had to pry her out of the car. The guy who caused the accident was drunk and only had a scratch on his face. He's sobering up in jail. The other two drivers are here in the hospital. They aren't as seriously hurt as Ms. Carter."

Was there any justice in this world?

"Is the boy going to need social services?" Sgt. Meraz asked.

"I'll take him. I served with Riley's brother in Iraq. We'll be there for him."

"Okay. Give me a number where I can reach you."

Tyler rattled off the number of the ranch.

After taking down the number, Sgt. Meraz added, "Ms. Carter's car was totaled." The sergeant told Tyler how to get the wrecked car and claim the things inside of it. "Here's my card. If you need anything, call me." Meraz handed Tyler his card, then walked out of the emergency room.

Tyler stared down at the card. Why had this happened? Why had God let this happen to Susan? The drunk walked away from the wreck without any major injuries, so where was the justice? Tyler closed his eyes and wanted to scream out his fury, but didn't want to scare the people in the emergency room. Besides, his losing it wouldn't help either Susan or Riley.

At the sound of the automatic doors opening, Beth and Riley looked up and saw Sgt. Meraz. He stopped and repeated his offer of help.

"Thank you," Beth whispered.

Silence settled around them. Riley stared down at his hands. "Why doesn't God like me?"

"What?" Beth stammered, reeling from the question.

When Riley looked up, his eyes were filled with pain. "First my dad. Then Paul. And now my mom," he whispered. "Maybe you shouldn't like me, because everyone who likes me is killed."

"Oh, no, Riley." Swallowing the lump in her throat, she pulled him into her arms and held him tight. "That's not true. God doesn't hate you."

"Then why?"

She scrambled to say something of comfort or be able to explain the unexplainable. Theologians and philosophers had wrestled with those same questions through the centuries. King David and King Solomon wrestled with those very issues in the Psalms and Proverbs. How could she answer this young man? What wisdom did she have?

Before Beth could begin to form an answer, Tyler appeared at the double doors. "The doctor wants to talk to us."

They hurried inside. The doctor was not anywhere to be seen. When Tyler walked to the desk, the doctor came out the emergency room doors.

"Doctor, here's Susan's son. Beth and I are friends of Susan."

The doctor looked at each person. "We're going

to take her into surgery now. Her spleen was ruptured, and she's broken both legs."

Beth wrapped her arm around Riley's shoulders.

The doctor continued, "We won't know if there's anything else wrong until we open her up." He looked at Riley. "Is your mom taking any medication? Or does she have any medical problems I should know about?"

"No. The only time she was in the hospital was when she had babies."

"Good. I'll come back and talk to you after we finish in surgery. There's a special waiting room. The nurse will show you where." He disappeared back through the double doors, again.

"Is she going to die?" Riley asked.

Tyler rested his hand on the boy's shoulder. "We don't know. We'll have to wait."

"And pray," Beth added.

The nurse appeared and led them to a waiting room on the fourth floor.

A TV was suspended in the corner of the waiting room. The morning network show was on. The program went from the network fed to local news. The perky little woman talked about the major wreck that happened this morning on Singing Arrow. Beth, Riley and Tyler looked at the TV. Beth stood up to change the station, but Riley put his hand on Beth's arm, stopping her from turning it off.

Beth looked at Tyler and silently questioned him. He nodded, agreeing with Riley.

They watched in horror as the reporter stood at the scene, explaining what happened. She interviewed one of the witnesses.

"That guy just sailed by the stop sign and there was no way the white car could avoid the wreck. It was real busy this morning and none of the cars had any time to stop running into the white car."

Riley collapsed into a chair. Beth and Tyler sat on either side of him.

Riley's earlier question about God kept running through Beth's brain. They sat silently for a half hour before she asked if he was hungry. He shook his head.

"You didn't answer my question," he finally muttered.

Beth's heart clenched.

Tyler leaned forward looking at them. "What did you ask?"

One shoulder lifted and went down. "I asked why God takes away all the people I love."

A muscle in Tyler's cheek jumped.

Beth grabbed Riley's right hand and held it between hers. "I know God doesn't hate you. Jesus died for you, so I don't think God is punishing you by killing your family. I don't know why things happen, but I do know God isn't punishing you. And He's not going to kill Tyler and me because we care for you."

"But there has to be a reason?" the boy demanded.

"Maybe there isn't. I remember when I was about seven, my parents had another child. It was another girl. April. She was about six months old and got a fever and nothing my parents, or the doctor, or the hospital did made any difference. She died.

"I didn't want April to die. My parents didn't want it, either, but it happened." Beth recalled the chubby infant with a sunny smile and infectious laugh. "After she died, I remember my mother sitting with her Bible in the empty nursery, singing nursery songs. I didn't understand it, but God didn't hate my parents. Sometimes I'd see my mother at the family graveyard, standing by April's grave and singing." She paused, surprised at the strength of the memory.

"But you know what?"

He shook his head.

"I remember April's blue eyes and my mother singing to her. I think my mother can remember her and thank Heaven that she had another little girl, if only for a moment. And I remember April as a little light of joy."

Riley considered Beth's words.

Tyler rested his elbows on his thighs and clasped his hands between his legs. "You remember me telling you that my parents died in a tornado?"

"Yeah."

"I wondered why they died. Afterward, I went to live with my grandmother. I lived with her a couple of years, then she died. There was no one, so the state got me." He fell silent. His entwined fingers twisted. "I went to some bad foster homes. And I got in a lot of trouble. I was mad, Riley. I asked the same questions, but I didn't get any answers.

"My last foster family let me be mad. And I pulled some stupid stunts, but they still loved me. I went to church with them and heard about Jesus. After I came to know Him, my heart had a peace. I had a new family that loved me. I wish my parents could've been with me, but I know they wouldn't have wanted me to be bitter and have my life filled with anger."

Riley's eyes filled with tears. "It's so hard." The flood of tears came and he leaned toward Tyler. He didn't hesitate and slipped his arm around the boy's shoulders.

Tears clouded Beth's eyes as she laid her hand on Riley's back.

They sat that way until Riley fell asleep.

Several hours later another group of people walked into the surgery waiting room. They nodded, but didn't say anything. Riley lay curled on the chair asleep. He'd finally given into the exhaustion that overwhelmed him. Staying up all night, plus the emotional upheaval, knocked him out. Tyler watched over Riley. He didn't know how Susan would fare, but Tyler knew that he would not abandon Riley. He could never replace Paul nor would he try, but he could be a friend and mentor to this young man.

God had sent him here.

The thought startled Tyler. He'd been so lost for so long, lost in his grief and guilt, he'd pushed away God. How could he bridge that gulf? But given this situation, he needed to figure it out.

Beth's stomach growled loud enough to draw him out of his thoughts.

Looking down at her stomach, Tyler said, "I think you need to feed that."

She covered her stomach with her hand. "I don't feel like it, but my body's saying differently." She looked at the clock on the wall. It was close to eleven-thirty. "She's been in there over four hours."

Tyler felt every moment of those hours. Covering her hand with his, he held it. "The doctor said it might take some time. Why don't you go and get us all something to eat. Riley might want something when he wakes. That's the beauty of youth, you can bounce back quickly."

"Okay, so what do you want?"

He hadn't eaten anything this morning, thinking he was about to go back to the ranch and crash. "It doesn't matter. But please bring coffee."

She disappeared out of the room.

Tyler's mind went back to the idea of being a friend and mentor to Riley. The idea clicked in his brain. If Paul couldn't be here, he could. But he would've preferred it was Paul who survived the blast and not him.

But if it had been Paul who survived, Tyler never would've meet Beth.

Beth. With her pushy ways and determined spirit. And green eyes and a smile that reflected heaven.

They'd called Zach and Sophie earlier from the hospital and Beth filled them in. He thought about having Zach bring Dogger to comfort Riley, but doubted the hospital would allow the dog to come in. Dogger had been his touchstone after Paul died, and Tyler knew the dog could help Riley in ways that no adult could.

Beth walked back into the waiting room. She noticed a new group of people sitting on the other side, and nodded to them. Beth carried a tray with two coffees, orange juice and several sandwiches, a bag of chips and cookies on it. She placed the tray on the table, pushing aside the magazines.

"I'll assume you are a man who like his coffee black. If you need some cream, I can get it."

"In the Army, you learn to like it black."

Beth walked to where the boy lay sleeping. "I brought him some chips and a couple of cookies. I don't know if he's going to want to eat, but it might keep him from worrying."

She sat next to Tyler and grabbed the other coffee and began to drink it.

"You were great with Riley's questions," Tyler whispered between sips of coffee.

She shook her head. "Talk about being caught flat-footed. I had no idea what to say. All I knew was that Riley was dead wrong. I scrambled to come up with an answer. You weren't so bad yourself."

He rubbed the back of his neck. "I didn't want Riley to think he was alone. I know what it feels like."

"You've got a gold star in your crown."

He drew back. "What are you talking about?"

"Haven't you ever heard that expression? When we get to heaven, you'll get a gold star in—"

"There you are, Beth," Sophie cried as she walked into the waiting room. Zach walked in behind her.

After hugs, Sophie asked, "Have you heard anything?"

"We're still waiting."

Riley moaned and opened his eyes. After scanning the room, he bolted straight up. He appeared embarrassed. "Is there any news?"

"Nothing so far." Beth pointed to the tray. "I brought you some orange juice and a sandwich if you're hungry."

He reached for the orange juice.

Sophie talked with Riley, getting him to tell her about the night. He automatically answered her questions.

Pastor Mike walked in the room. Tyler moved and Pastor Mike sat beside Riley.

"We're here for you, Riley. I called several of the teens and we're all praying for your mom." He looked at Beth. "If there's anything the church can do, we want to help."

"Thanks," Beth said.

"Why don't we pray now?" Pastor asked.

The group huddled around Riley and joined hands. Pastor quietly led the prayer, but Beth finished it.

"…and strengthen Susan, help the doctors and touch Riley's heart with comfort and peace. Amen."

"Amen," the group repeated.

Riley nodded. "Thanks," he mumbled.

A doctor came in and talked quietly to the others in the waiting room. "He's not dead," the woman screamed.

The room went silent as the woman started crying. The man beside her pulled her into his arms and they followed the doctor out of the room.

A heavy silence hung in the air, nearly suffocating them. Riley bolted to his feet and left the room. Beth exited after him. Tyler followed. Riley stood by a window that looked out over the parking lot.

"What am I going to do?" he whispered.

Tyler rested his hand on Riley's shoulder. "I'll be here for you."

"None of us will desert you," Beth reassured him. "But let's wait to hear what the doctor says."

A flicker of hope entered his eyes.

The doctor appeared in the hall. He still had on his blue surgical cap, scrubs and shoe covers.

"How is she?" Beth asked.

The doctor motioned for them to go into the waiting room before him. He settled on the coffee table across from Riley and Beth. "You're mom is out of surgery."

A tear rolled down the boy's cheek. Beth slipped her arm around his shoulders. "So she's going to be all right?"

"Well, she's alive and came through the surgery well." He looked at Beth and Tyler. "We removed her spleen. She broke both legs and had several broken ribs. She won't be returning to work any time soon."

"But she's okay," Riley asked again.

Beth could see the doctor choosing his words carefully.

"Your mother's alive, but she does have some major injuries."

Riley nodded.

"We're going to keep her in ICU probably for the rest of the day just to keep a close eye on her. Any questions?"

"Can Riley see his mother for a moment?" Beth asked.

"I think that can be arranged. She'll be in recovery for a while, then moved to ICU in the late afternoon. Check with the nurse later."

The doctor left.

Sophie hugged Beth and Riley. After a brief prayer of thanks Sophie, Zach and Pastor Mike left.

A couple of hours later, the nurse appeared, calling for the relatives of Susan Carter. Since Riley was so young, he was allowed to have someone with him when he visited his mother. He asked Tyler to come with him.

"Two minutes," the nurse warned. She looked at Riley. "Don't let all the tubes and machines scare you. She's waking up from a deep sleep, and she's coming along just fine."

Riley walked slowly toward his mother. He hesitated, taking in her battered body. He looked up at the nurse. "Can I touch her?"

"Yes, just be careful not to pull any of the tubes."

The boy touched his mother's left hand. "Hi, Mom." His voice quivered. "You got banged up pretty bad in the accident, but you're going to be okay. Don't worry about me. I'm going to stay at the ranch with Tyler. And Dogger and Prince Charming. So you hurry up and get well." Riley looked over his shoulder to Tyler. "She's going to be okay, right?"

How did he answer without lying? "Everyone in this hospital is going to work to help her."

Riley turned back to his mother. "And we're going to pray, Mom, that you're going to get well."

The words hit Tyler in the heart. "We are."

Beth stood in the ICU waiting room, looking out the windows at the courtyard below. It was done in a traditional Southwestern motif, with big mason jugs piled on each other and a waterfall from one jug to another. An adobe bench with mosaic tiles covering the seat. A matching covered bench sat in the corner with vines growing up the wooden pillars holding up the overhead lattice.

She tried to still her raging thoughts and crushing worry. "Lord, please bring Susan through this. Help Riley," she whispered.

Tyler had been a steady presence in the past few hours. She saw him in a new light. When the chips were down, he was a man who didn't walk away from the situation.

In the background, the early afternoon news came on, with the number-one story being the wreck this morning. Beth grabbed the remote and turned off the set. Riley didn't need to walk in on that.

Beth's cell phone rang. Digging though her purse, she found her phone and answered.

"Hey, sis, how are things going there at the hospital? Zach called to let me know what happened. Do I need to come down there?" Beth's older brother asked.

"No, Ethan. There's nothing you can do but pray. Susan made it through surgery. Riley's in there with his mom now."

"What about Riley or Tyler? You think that Zach will need another hand at the ranch this afternoon?"

"I don't know. Call him, see how things are going."

"Have you called Susan's work, letting them know what happened?"

"No. That's a good idea. Thanks, Ethan."

"Call if you need anything."

When Beth hung up, she called Sophie and got the number for Susan's work and called them.

"You mean that story I heard this morning going to work was Susan?" Susan's boss replied. "She said she might be a little late, but we never thought—" After a tense moment, she added, "Thanks for letting us know."

"Susan's at UNM hospital if you want to come by," Beth told the woman. "By tomorrow she'll probably be in a private room."

The instant she finished, Riley and Tyler walked into the room.

The fear in the boy's eyes cut into her heart. Beth pulled him into her arms. He didn't resist. Beth looked into Tyler's eyes.

"Susan's in serious condition."

"She looks so helpless," Riley whispered.

Beth pulled back. "But she's alive and has a fighting chance."

Riley didn't look convinced.

"Let's go back to the ranch and get some sleep. Your mom needs us rested before she sees us. It will make her feel better if she sees you looking well," Tyler said.

A flicker of hope danced in Riley's expression. "Really?"

"Tyler's right," Beth added. "The best thing we can do now is to go back to the ranch and sleep."

"Okay."

As they walked out of the hospital, Beth touched Tyler's arm. "Thank you," she whispered.

He nodded.

Riding back to the ranch, Beth's last thought before she slipped into a light sleep was that Tyler was a man of honor.

Chapter Twelve

By the time they arrived at the ranch, Riley was sound asleep, slumped against Beth, who also was out like a light. Riley staggered out the driver's side of the truck and into the foreman's house. He fell fully clothed onto the bed in the first bedroom. Beth's eyes fluttered open when Tyler came back to the car.

"My car's at the church," she mumbled when Tyler opened the passenger side of the truck.

"I think you need a nap before you drive anywhere."

She didn't move, only gave him a sleepy smile. "Yeah, you're right. Come back in a little while."

"You can crash in my room."

Her eyes widened.

"I'll sleep on the couch," he hastily added.

Her eyes drifted closed and she shook her head and wagged her right forefinger at him. "No can do. I'll crash at my brother's place. Give me a minute before I walk up there." Her hand flopped onto the bench seat. She frowned and pulled something up in her hand.

"What's this?" she mumbled, holding up the plastic-wrapped fried pie. She opened one eye.

Tyler's face flushed. "It's a coconut fried pie. I bought it for you."

She rolled her head on the seatback toward him and smiled. "That's nice." Her eyes fluttered closed and a soft snore left her mouth.

Tyler laughed, shaking his head. He gathered her in his arms and started up to the main house.

"I can walk," she mumbled into his neck.

A chuckle rumbled through his chest. "I know, but I'd like to go to sleep, too, so I figured it would be faster this way."

"You're funny." Her left arm snaked around his neck and her right hand clutched the fried pie to her stomach. She rested her head under his chin. "You smell good," she mumbled.

"That's the fried pie. Someone sat on it."

She shook her head. "No. It's you."

He didn't bother to answer.

"You smell real good, and you're strong and handsome, too," she whispered into his neck.

Her breath tickled. "Thank you."

"I thought you were stuck-up when I first saw you, but—"

He waited to hear what she thought.

"I—I wondered what you looked like when you smiled."

"You did?"

"Yeah, and you know what? When you did smile, you were dreamy." She smiled and slipped into a deep sleep.

He'd been called a lot of things, but dreamy? Tyler moved up the walk to the main house. Ollie saw him.

"What are you doing?"

"Putting Sleeping Beauty to bed."

Ollie shook his head and went back into the stables.

As Tyler climbed the front steps of the house, the screen door opened and Sophie and another older woman stepped out. Sophie's eyebrow arched.

"The night's caught up with her. She didn't want to sleep at the foreman's house, but said she'd crash here, only she's never been awake long enough to walk up here by herself."

"I can see that. Margaret, I'll be back in a moment. Come in, Tyler, and I'll show you where to put her." Sophie opened the screen and led him down the hall to what he guessed was a guest bedroom. He laid Beth on the bed and they took off her shoes. Tyler gently took the fried pie out of her hand and put it on the nightstand. Sophie threw him a look, but he didn't explain about the pie. He'd bought that for Beth because—because he wanted to surprise her with that little gift.

Sophie didn't question him about it, but put a blanket over her friend. "How's Riley?"

"He's sound asleep at my place."

"I don't doubt that. You need to get some sleep yourself. I know your combat experience helps you, but you need the rest."

He felt his sleep coming on and agreed with Sophie.

She motioned to him. "Come and meet the last owner of the ranch."

Tyler followed Sophie out onto the porch. An older woman was by the stables talking to Ollie. From what Tyler could see, they knew each other well.

"Margaret owned the ranch for close to forty years before she sold it to me. I used to ride here when I was a teen." Sophie motioned to the two. "Ollie's worked here for nearly thirty years."

The wind carried Margaret's words. "I like my apartment in the retirement center. I don't have to worry if the stock is fed and watered or if we'll have enough money to continue."

Ollie nodded, but his eyes never left Margaret's face. "Sophie and Zach are running things well. Lots of new folks and Army vets. You'd be proud."

Tyler looked at Sophie to gauge her reaction to the praise. Her chin came up and her eyes sparkled.

Turning back, he saw Margaret smile at Ollie, but the left corner of her mouth didn't go up. "Come by and see me again, Ollie. I enjoyed dinner. You know I'm not driving, but that doesn't stop me. And it shouldn't stop you."

They traded looks.

Sophie leaned close to Tyler. "I always wondered if they had a thing for each other."

Margaret turned and walked back to the porch. She had a slight limp.

Sophie introduced them. "Margaret just came by to visit and see how things were progressing here. I think she heard I was pregnant and nothing was going to stop her."

"I told the people at the retirement center to bring me here or I'd escape."

"Sounds like you." Sophie turned to Tyler. "After I was discharged, I knew I wanted to start the equine therapy for soldiers after I saw some of the guys I treated riding in Iraq and making amazing progress. When I came by to see Margaret, I discussed it with her. She loved the idea and knew it would help her granddaughter who has Downs, so we launched the program for kids and worked to set up the program for vets."

Tyler nodded. "Ma'am. It's nice to meet you. I wish I could stay a little longer and talk, but I spent the night at the lock-in with teens and have been at the hospital most of the day. I can't guarantee how much longer I'll make any sense."

"Go." Sophie shooed him away.

"Nice to meet you, Tyler."

"Same here."

Sophie glowed. Tyler wondered if all women did that when they were pregnant or was it only because Sophie was so happy. He wondered how Beth would look.

He stumbled. Whoa. He clamped down on the thought. Marriage and babies. He really was tired.

And yet, the idea took root and he liked it.

Entering his house, he checked on Riley. Tyler moved to the bed and took off the kid's shoes. Dogger had settled bedside on the floor.

"You going to keep watch over the boy?"

Dogger looked up at Tyler, then closed his eyes. That was fine with Tyler. Dogger had more sense than a lot of folks he knew.

As he settled in his bed in the back room, his mind went to what Beth had mumbled as he carried her up to the main house. She thought he was dreamy. He'd never had a woman tell him that, but kind of liked that idea.

They were on patrol. The tiny village looked deserted. The intel they possessed indicated this village was a bomb-making hot spot.

"Found it," Paul called out.

Tyler slipped into the house. The first room stood empty, the cooking fire in the corner of the room cold. As Tyler started though the second door to the back room, he heard Dogger growl. The dog had followed them from the truck. Dogger's hackles stood up, and Tyler knew something wasn't right.

"Paul, you okay?"

"There's C-4 and sticks of dynamite and nails in here."

Dogger continued to growl.

"Somethin's not right. The dog's on alert. Look around."

Paul didn't respond. Finally, he whispered, "It's booby-trapped. Get out."

Tyler turned and ran out the front door just as the house blew up, knocking him to the ground, forcing the air out of his lungs. After several minutes, Dogger licked his face, whining. "Paul," Tyler cried out. He staggered to his feet and ran around the back of the house. Paul lay sprawled on the ground. Tyler rolled him to his side, looking for any wounds.

"Paul?"

Tyler saw the beat of his friend's heart in his neck. Tyler poured water in his hand and wiped the dust off of Paul's face. He choked and his eyes fluttered open. Paul's grin wasn't far behind. He *looked at Dogger and said, "I think our mascot deserves a medal, and I'm going to put in for him."*

Tyler jerked awake, his heart pounding. He sat on the bed, his head cradled in his hands. Just when he thought his heart had made peace with the ghosts of the past and he'd started to hope for the future, he was back in Iraq.

Dogger looked up at him.

Tyler petted his head. "I don't think you ever got a medal, boy, but you deserve one."

There was no point in going back to sleep. He went to the bathroom and splashed water on his face. He needed to shave, but he had no desire to shave this late in the day.

Moving to the front bedroom, he checked on Riley. He still slept peacefully. What would the boy think if he knew the true circumstances surrounding Paul's death? Would Riley hate him?

Tyler walked out to the barn. The last riders and volunteers drove out of the parking lot. Walking into the stables, Ollie nodded to him.

"Good, you're up. I could use some help."

They were welcome words. If Tyler were busy, he might be able to ignore his dream and the memories they brought. At least he could hope it would.

But he knew it wouldn't work.

* * *

Beth slowly woke. Looking around the room, she recognized the guest room in her brother's house. On the nightstand, she saw something in plastic wrap. Her brain fought to make sense of it. The light coming in the windows told her it was late in the day. How did she get here?

"Oh, no." She threw off the afghan and her feet hit the floor. Then raced to the bathroom, rinsed out her mouth, and washed her face. After finishing up, she ran back to the bedroom. Reaching for the fried pie, she worked off the plastic on one end and pulled off a pinch of the pie and popped it into her mouth.

Oh, the wonderful taste. Now she needed a cup of coffee. She pulled on her shoes and grabbed the fried pie and headed out of the room. Tyler had bought her a fried pie—a coconut fried pie. He remembered her favorite. That told her more about his feelings than a dozen roses. She wanted to find Tyler and give him a kiss.

The thought stopped her. Looking down at the fried pie, her feeling overwhelmed her. Had she'd fallen in love? After so many years of avoiding committing her heart, a mutt and a pensive man with a fried pie got to her. Who would've thought that was the way to her heart?

Thinking of all that happened last night, it had

been a roller coaster ride from the high of Tyler holding her hand to the low of Susan's accident.

As she thought about them coming back from the hospital— Oh, mercy, what had she said to him as he carried her up to the main house? She vaguely remembered saying something about him being strong and—

"So you're finally awake." Sophie stood in the hall, eating a cookie.

Beth stopped short. "What time is it?"

"After seven. Your brother and I are finishing up dinner. If you're hungry, you can join us." Sophie looked at the fried pie. "What do you have there?"

Beth smiled at her friend. "A fried pie."

"You're looking at it as if it was a diamond."

Beth's mouth trembled. "It's as valuable to me."

Sophie moved to her friend's side. "You're in love."

Sucking in her lips, Beth struggled with hearing the truth Sophie just announced. It was one thing to think that thought to herself. It was another to openly admit it to another person. "Well, I think— Oh, I don't…"

Sophie wrapped her arms around her friend. "I've watched you over the years avoid commitments to different men. You were never overt or nasty in anything, but you kept those men at arm's distance.

"I don't know how you were burned, and I'm not sure if your family really understands why there's not a boyfriend, but I know it's time to trust your heart, friend. It's lonely if you keep love at bay. I know. I've seen it from both sides. It's much nicer when you give in and trust your heart."

Sophie's words vibrated in Beth's heart, but she wasn't ready to acknowledge the truth her friend spoke. These new feelings were still too fragile to share. Beth hugged her friend. "Thank you."

She started toward the kitchen. "Do you know how Susan is doing? Have you talked any more to Tyler? Do you know where he is?"

Sophie caught her hand and pulled her to a stop. "I haven't heard."

"I need to see if Tyler knows anything."

"You, friend, need something in your stomach to make your brain function. And from your incoherent answers thus far, I'd say you need to eat."

"I don't have time."

"You need some protein."

Beth's mouth opened to protest.

"Remember, we were roomies. I remember how you get when you're hungry. C'mon, I've got pot roast, potatoes and biscuits."

Beth's stomach growled, making her grin. "Okay."

They walked into the kitchen to find Zach gathering the dishes. Beth stopped and took in the scene. Her mouth nearly fell open.

"If I hadn't seen it with my own eyes, I wouldn't have believed it. Mom won't believe it, either."

"Funny."

Sophie headed toward the stove. "I'll fix you a plate. Zach, why don't you pour your sister some coffee?"

Much to Beth's surprise, Zach followed his wife's directions and poured her a cup of coffee. Both Sophie and Zach sat down with her.

Beth put down the fried pie and took a sip of coffee. "Have you heard anything about how Susan's doing?"

"No," Zach replied. "And things have been quiet down at the foreman's house. Several of the pastors and members of the church have called, asking how things are."

Beth reached for a biscuit. It tasted wonderful.

"I think it might be a good idea to fix a couple of plates for Tyler and Riley. When I'm finished here, I'll take them over." And she could talk to Tyler to see if her memory of her ramblings was accurate. And test out the budding feelings she'd finally acknowledged, if only to herself.

"Done," Sophie said.

Beth frowned.

"I already took the boys something earlier. Riley was still asleep, but Tyler was up," Zach said.

"How's he doing?"

"Okay." But Zach's face had closed down and Beth knew from his look that no matter how much she questioned Zach, he wouldn't give her any more information. Still, something wasn't right.

As she finished her dinner, scenes from last night kept playing in her head: Tyler and Riley laughing, playing pinball, bumper cars, Riley bowling. Beth knew this was the first time since his brother had been killed that Riley'd had fun, so what had happened to Susan had been even more devastating. From joy to weeping, they'd been on an emotional roller coaster.

She put her plate in the sink and picked up the phone and called the hospital.

She asked for ICU. The charge nurse told her that Susan's condition had improved and she would be moved to a semiprivate room later tonight. Hanging up, Beth turned and told Sophie and Zach what she'd learned.

"That's wonderful news." Sophie hugged Beth.

"I have to tell Tyler." She grabbed her fried pie.

As she passed Zach, he reached out and pulled her into his arms. "Go gently," he whispered into her hair.

The hairs on the back of Beth's neck rose. Pulling back, she looked into her brother's eyes, trying to make sense of his warning. "Why?"

He smoothed some of her curls back from her face. "Pray while you're dealing with Tyler and Riley."

"Okay. Is there something you want to tell me?"

"Just walk softly. People sometimes have odd reactions to a traumatic event. Remember how mom and dad reacted to me losing my leg? They didn't deal well with it."

"Okay." Warily, she headed toward the foreman's house. Zach had tried to tell her something, but what?

Looking out over the practice rings, she saw that all was calm. Beth's heart raced with anticipation as she walked toward the house. She wished she remembered Tyler's reaction to her comments when he carried her to the house. What on earth had possessed her to run her mouth and say those revealing things?

Pushing aside her embarrassment, she thought of Riley and Susan. She and Tyler would need to come up with a plan to deal with the day-to-day living and caring for the two. This was not the time to worry about her pride.

The front door was open, but the screen was closed. She knocked. "Tyler." After several moments, when he didn't appear, she tried the screen door. It opened easily. Walking inside, she called

Tyler's name. In the kitchen, two plates sat on the table.

Why hadn't Tyler eaten? Was he still asleep? That couldn't be. Zach said he was awake. She walked back through the house. In the first bedroom, Riley lay on the bed, asleep.

She quietly backed out of the room. She looked in the other rooms. Tyler wasn't in the house. Walking to the front door, she spied Dogger on the porch. Opening the door, she squatted down and stroked Dogger's head. "Hey, guy. Where's your owner?"

The dog rolled over and allowed her to scratch his belly. "You're no help. I need to find Tyler." She scanned the practice rings and stables but there was no sign of him. The setting sun bathed the landscape in gold and red, making the world seem enchanted and at peace.

Dogger rolled to his feet and started toward the stables. He stopped and looked over his shoulder.

"Okay, I'm coming."

The dog waited until she caught up with him and trotted into the stables. He headed toward the tack room and disappeared inside.

"Hey, boy, where have you been?" Tyler's voice floated out of the room.

Beth moved to the door and watched as Tyler petted his dog. When he looked up from where he sat on the overturned barrel, he saw Beth.

"Hi." Suddenly Beth felt shy, remembering her rambling monologue.

"You rested?"

"I am. Before I got out of the house, Sophie made sure I ate. She's got food for you, too, on the table."

He nodded. "It must be the mother instinct in her coming out."

"You need to remember she was an Army medic, so the woman has a caring streak."

"I remember."

"You want to go and eat your dinner?"

He didn't answer. Something was wrong. He had closed down again. She searched for something to say. "Riley's still asleep."

"Good. He needs that."

It was as if the past few weeks had evaporated, and he'd used up all the joy and smiles in his soul. She moved into the room. Standing by his side, she asked, "What's wrong, Tyler?"

"Aside from the fact that Riley almost lost his mother?"

She knelt by the barrel he sat on. "But he didn't."

He looked away from her. "What would've happened if he had? There's no other relatives to take care of him, thanks to me."

He wasn't making any sense. "What are you talking about?"

"It's my fault that Paul's dead."

His words felt like a neutron bomb, killing all the living things in the world, but sparing all the equipment and material in the room. "What are you talking about?"

"It's my fault Paul's dead." His gaze locked with hers, and she knew in the depth of her soul he meant exactly what he said.

"That can't be right."

"It is." His gaze turned inward. "I should've died that day instead of Paul."

She grasped his hand between hers. "Why do you say that?"

"Paul and I were called to a café near the green zone. One of our guys spotted a bomb under one of the tables and they called us. My team was dispatched to disarm it. The bomb was composed of sticks of dynamite, surrounded by nails. It looked like it had a timer on it. Paul started to disarm it, and I'd just turned to get the wire cutter from my bag. Before I could turn back, the bomb exploded. Paul caught it in the face and throat." Tyler's eyes went black with pain. The weight of what had happened crushed him.

"The timer was a decoy. The bomber was in the restaurant, waiting for the Americans to disarm it."

She'd noticed the scars on Tyler's forearms and one at the base of his neck. She kissed the back of his hand where there was a scar. "I'm so sorry, Tyler."

They heard a noise in the barn outside of the tack room. Beth stood and walked to the door, looking around the stables. No one was there. Dogger trotted past her and disappeared into the dark. Beth went back to Tyler and knelt by him.

"I looked Paul in the eyes while the life leaked out of him." He choked back tears. "I should've been the one to die. I was his commander. Paul had family who needed him. I d—"

She wrapped her arms around his neck. He buried his face in her neck and pulled her close. His body shook as the sorrow and grief poured out of him.

His pain washed over her and she, in turn, prayed for this wounded soul. "Oh, Tyler." She stroked his back, knowing this was probably the first time he'd vented his grief. She didn't know how long she held him, but slowly he became still.

He drew back. His eyes still held sadness, but the devastating bleakness was gone. "Grown men aren't supposed to do that."

"Says who?"

He didn't answer.

"It will be our secret. I don't think Prince Charming will spill the beans. He's pretty good at keeping secrets."

"So I hear."

She tried getting to her feet, but her legs weren't

cooperating. Her lower left leg had gone to sleep. Tyler stood and helped her to her feet.

"Who would've thought at the age of twenty-nine, I'd be moving so slowly."

"That must make me ancient at thirty-five."

She grinned. "You said it, not me."

He smiled back at her, and Beth felt her spirit lift. Maybe he needed to vent that grief before his soul could heal.

They checked the horses before they left the stables. Beth patted Charming on the nose. "Hey, big guy, have you seen Dogger?"

Charming ignored her and went back to sleep.

"I wonder if Riley's still sleeping," Beth said. "I'd like to say goodbye to him and tell him the news about his mom. If you'll drive me back to the church to get my car, we might be able to stop by the hospital and see Susan."

"Sounds good to me."

They walked up the porch stairs. Beth stared to reach for the door, but Tyler caught her hand, pulling her around to face him.

"Thank you." He brushed a lock of her hair behind her ear. He tipped her chin up and covered her mouth with his.

Beth eagerly returned the kiss.

When he drew back, he smiled at her.

"Was that a thank-you?"

"No. That was what I wanted to do last night and didn't have the opportunity."

"Well, I'm glad you gave in to the urge." Her heart filled with joy and hope. Something that hadn't been there since the slap her ex-boyfriend had delivered. She leaned up and gave him another kiss.

When they broke apart, she said, "That was for the fried pie. That's probably one of the most thoughtful gifts I've gotten."

The man blushed. Actually blushed. She enjoyed the sight. "It seemed like a good thing at the time."

She patted him on the arm. "It was."

"Let's go inside and wake up Riley, feed him and go to the hospital."

She wanted another kiss, but pushed away the thought and nodded.

He opened the door and motioned Beth inside. They walked to the bedroom where Riley slept but the room was empty.

"He might be in the kitchen," Beth offered.

Tyler went to the bed and put his hand on the messed up covers. "They're cold."

In the kitchen Riley's plate sat untouched. He wasn't in the bathroom, either. They quickly searched the house, but there was no sign of him.

Beth met Tyler's eyes. "That noise."

"He heard. He knows how his brother died and he ran away."

"You don't know that."

He didn't bother answering. It was there in the despair in his eyes.

Chapter Thirteen

They split up. Beth ran to the main house to alert Zach and Sophie, while Tyler went to the stables. As she ran to the main house, Beth's heart pounded in panic. What had Riley heard? She barged into her brother's house. "Riley's gone."

Sophie and Zach looked up from the sofa where they sat side by side, watching the TV.

Zach released his wife's hand. "What are you talking about?"

"Tyler and I were in the tack room. He was upset about Susan's accident. He said some stuff we think Riley may have overheard. And now he's gone."

Zach stood. "You searched the foreman's house?"

"Yes, but he wasn't there. Tyler's down at the stables looking through the stalls, but I don't think he's going to find him there."

"You and Sophie take the truck and see if you can spot him. I'll join Tyler. We have some ATVs and we can use them to search." He walked into the kitchen and grabbed a couple of flashlights. He also pulled out the walkie-talkies he kept in the mud room. "Take the other one and keep in contact with us."

Sophie nodded. Zach walked out of the house.

"I'll get my keys and we can start our search."

Beth closed her eyes as the misery washed over her. She feared that if something happened to Riley, Tyler's heart would completely shut down. *Lord, keep Riley safe, for his sake. And Tyler's.*

Sophie touched Beth's shoulder. Beth opened her eyes.

"We'll find him."

"Yes, we will."

They headed out to the truck.

Shoving aside his fear, Tyler searched the stables and checked each stall, but didn't find signs of the kid. Zach showed up as he finished the last stall.

Zach glanced around. "Have you finished searching the building?"

"Yeah. He's not here."

"Are any of the horses missing?"

Tyler hadn't thought of that. "No, all the horses are here, but—" Suddenly he realized he hadn't seen Dogger, then remembered how the dog had slipped out of the tack room after they heard the noise in the hall.

Tyler staggered over to the half wall and leaned against it. "Dogger is with Riley."

"How do you know that?"

"That dog's got an instinct that's beyond anything I can understand. He knows. And he saved me and the other guys in our unit more than once, alerting us to danger, so I don't doubt that Dogger's with Riley, no matter where he is."

"Okay, if the boy didn't take a horse, he couldn't have gone far on foot. How long has he been missing?"

Tyler racked his brain. "It couldn't be more than twenty minutes."

"All right. Let's start looking around the ranch. I've got a jeep and some ATVs we can use to search."

Tyler didn't even want to think how Riley had reacted to his confession and how much of what he said Riley had actually heard. How could he have been so stupid? "Let's do it."

Zach and Tyler got the ATVs out and started searching the river area on the far edge of the ranch. Sophie and Beth took the truck and went to the closest neighboring ranch. Sophie called Ollie and let him know what was happening. Ollie drove back to the ranch to babysit the ranch office. He would try to coordinate things if they needed to call the sheriff's office. They kept in contact with walkie-talkies.

Sophie and Beth first drove to the neighbors north of their ranch. Together they'd searched the barns and outbuildings but didn't find any sign of Riley. "Carol, please keep looking out for the teen. He's probably not thinking too clearly with what happened to his mother, but our hope is he's hungry and thirsty and will show up somewhere."

"You let me know if you find him. Bob and I will keep watch, and if you need for us to search tomorrow, we will. I wouldn't want him to spend the night outside. It's going to be in the low fifties tonight."

"I promise we'll let you know if we find him."

She and Beth walked back to the car. "You drive," Sophie told Beth. "I'll call the other ranches and have them start looking."

Beth climbed behind the steering wheel while Sophie slid into the passenger seat. Buckling up, Sophie grabbed her cell phone and started calling. Beth tried to concentrate on the road and watch for signs of Riley, but she had to fight off her fear.

After her last call, Sophie rested her hand on Beth's arm. Sophie was one of the few people who could really read Beth's mood. Most folks just saw the chipper, bubbly woman. "It's not your fault, Beth."

"I shouldn't have pushed Tyler so hard. I had to know why he was in a funk. I just couldn't leave it alone. I had to understand." She took a deep breath to steady herself. "The night had gone so well, Sophie. We were riding so high. Riley and Tyler laughed and talked. Riley and one of the girls in the youth group spent the night sitting next to each other, smiling and trading looks. And when the kids conducted the service, I saw both Tyler and Riley pay attention. There was a hunger in both of their eyes. Riley had even weathered his mother's wreck and I think he was going to be okay. He had hope—"

Gripping the steering wheel, she felt the remorse wash through her. "I wanted to help, but it backfired on me. Big time." Her throat clogged with emotions.

"You didn't cause Susan's wreck, nor did you have anything to do with Tyler's issue. When Zach and I ran into him at the restaurant in the city last May, he carried that bruised look I've seen too many times on Zach's face and other soldiers I've dealt with. I knew Tyler carried a deep burden. Zach recognized it, too, and neither one of us could walk away from him."

"He certainly was off-putting when he first got

here. And I recognized that look, too. That's why last night was so great."

"What did he say that caused Riley to flee?"

Beth explained about the situation with the bomb and that Riley had overheard Tyler's admission. "Tyler feels he should've been the one disarming the bomb, and it should've been he who died."

Sophie nodded and looked out the window, searching for Riley. "Survivor's guilt," she whispered. "It's a wicked thing that ties up a person's soul. I saw it in a lot of the guys who survived an ambush or who dodged a bullet but their fellow unit members didn't." She fell silent. "I had it, and it had nothing to do with Iraq."

Beth reached over and grasped Sophie's hand. Beth knew her friend blamed herself for her brother's death. It had been a tragic accident that Sophie's family hadn't come to grips with for many years.

Tyler and Riley emerged from their sorrow, only to be thrust back into the shadows. *Why, Lord, why? Why had it happened? What good is served here?*

When they arrived at the next ranch, the family had finished a search of the barn and Riley wasn't there. As they drove to the next ranch, Sophie checked in with Ollie. No news. Riley seemed to have fallen off the face of the earth.

Close to midnight they returned to the ranch. Sophie needed to rest. They didn't want anything to happen to the baby she carried.

Tyler and Zach sat in the family room. From their expressions, Beth knew they'd found no sign of the boy. She walked to the phone and called the hospital to check on Susan's condition. Susan's vitals were strong. She'd woken up, but quickly gone back to sleep.

Beth gave the group a report on Susan. "At least she won't wonder about her son."

Her words wouldn't comfort Tyler.

Zach stood. "We need to notify the police. I'll call the sheriff right now." He dialed the sheriff at home. After a brief conversation, Zach said, "Okay, I'll see you tomorrow at sunrise. And you'll bring the volunteer rescue group?" He thanked the sheriff and hung up, turning to the group. "We'll start the search here tomorrow morning at sunrise. Try to sleep. You'll need to be alert tomorrow."

Sophie wrapped her arms around her husband's waist. "Beth, why don't you stay in the guest room again? You can borrow some of my prepregnancy things."

Beth thought about it. It would make life easier than having Tyler drive her to the church. Besides, she didn't want to leave at this critical point and she knew Tyler didn't want to leave, either.

"Sounds good."

"I'll grab you a couple of things. And pray for Riley." After their good-nights, Zach and Sophie left the room.

Tyler sat in silence across from Beth. He couldn't hide his pain and guilt. She wanted to reach out to him, but knew he wouldn't accept her efforts.

"I'll need to notify my boss I won't be in tomorrow." She had a business trip in a couple of days that she couldn't miss.

Zach appeared in the doorway with several items of clothing. He gave them to Beth. He kissed her cheek, nodded to Tyler and left.

"Dogger's with him. Surely he'll take care of Riley."

Tyler raised his head. "Dogger will guard him from night predators."

"And will keep him warm."

"Yes. But he shouldn't be out there. How is driving away my friend's brother caring for him?"

"You didn't—"

"Don't." He raised his hand. "Don't justify my mistakes." Standing, he stalked out of the house.

Beth stared at the door. Her eyes fluttered closed and she fought the pain. Her heart had opened up and now—

Lord, we need Your grace. And mercy. Bless Riley.
And Tyler.
Only You can save this situation.

Riley huddled among the rocks on the side of
the hill. Several trees grew farther up the slope,
but huddling out in the open had more appeal to
him. The boulders were still warm from the heat
of the day and he welcomed that heat. Dogger
curled against his side, protecting him from the
breeze and any of the animals creeping in the
dark.

He heard the howl of a coyote.

"I'm glad you're here with me, guy," Riley told
Dogger, putting his arm over the dog.

Riley rested his head against the large boulder.
His stomach rumbled. He rubbed it. He should've
eaten that plate of food on the table before he took
off, but he felt so good when he woke up and
wanted to talk to either Tyler or Beth about the
night and ask how his mother was doing. And if
she was really going to be okay. He thought they
could all eat together like a family.

He also wanted to know how things were going
to work after his mother got out of the hospital.
She wouldn't be able to care for herself, let alone
him. He could make sandwiches and wash his
clothes, but how would he get to school, or take

his mother to the doctor or get groceries? What if something happened to his mom? That thought scared him.

Why had that accident happened? Things were just looking up. He'd had fun staying up all night and making new friends who thought he was cool. It had been the first time he'd had a good time since Paul died.

He'd laughed. Last night had been super, and he'd wanted to ask Beth about going to church again. He'd wanted to talk to Tyler about girls. And it had been fun to watch Tyler stealing looks at Beth and how she blushed.

He remembered his brother and the good times they'd had, and how he could talk to Tyler about Paul. They'd been friends in the Army.

When Riley didn't find anyone in the house, he went outside, hoping to find someone. Tyler's car was there. Riley went to the stables, thinking that maybe Tyler was feeding the horses. When he heard voices, he hurried toward them, eager to talk. As he neared the tack room door, he heard what Tyler was saying. He paused, to listen more.

He should've died instead of Paul.

Riley froze, not sure he heard the words correctly. He struggled to understand. Tyler claimed it was his fault Paul died. His fault. And he should've died instead of Paul.

Riley stood there thunderstruck. What was Tyler talking about? When the light came on in Riley's brain, he couldn't stand the truth and ran.

No wonder Tyler wanted to help him. He felt guilty.

Guilty.

Riley didn't know where he was going, but he wouldn't spend another minute near Tyler. His anger and hurt drove him, his legs pumping, trying to outrace the words. When the adrenaline faded, he looked around the landscape. He had no idea where he was. That frightened him.

Thinking he'd find the highway and could thumb a ride, he started walking. When Dogger appeared at his side, Riley tried to send him away, but the dog wouldn't leave. And secretly, Riley was grateful Dogger didn't go.

So, he was lost in the middle of nowhere. What was he going to do?

Riley lay down, curling his body around the dog.

At least Dogger could be depended on.

And what would happen if his mother didn't live?

The thought scared him.

Before sunrise, Sophie walked among the group of searchers, pouring coffee into the foam cups. She also had warm muffins for anyone who was hungry.

Sheriff Joe Teague looked at the volunteers and his deputies. "You all have a description of the boy. He's traveling with a black-and-white dog."

"The dog's name is Dogger," Beth offered. She turned to Tyler. "Will Dogger allow the searchers near Riley?"

"I think so." He moved up to the inside of the circle. "Dogger went with Riley for his protection. Just call out to Riley and tell him you are part of the search party. Dogger is a protective animal and he is very aware of people approaching him."

Sheriff Joe nodded. "Now each of you has a partner. Stay within view of each other. Make sure you have your water and energy food bars. The boy will be hungry when you find him. Any other questions?"

No other questions emerged, and the group went different ways. Some of the searchers were on foot, with dogs, and others were on horseback. All had emergency walkie-talkies.

Beth moved to the barn, intent on saddling Prince Charming. Zach and Tyler followed her.

"Beth, are you sure you don't want to take the ATV?" Zach asked.

"No. Charming and I will ride out east of the ranch. There's a dirt road, maybe Riley followed that." The dirt road ran close to the river.

"I should ride Charming," Zach said. "You take Brownie."

Beth was small enough it wouldn't be a strain for her to ride the smaller horse. "Okay."

Tyler moved to Dusty's stall. "I'll saddle Dusty and ride out with you, Beth." He looked like death, and Beth knew he probably hadn't slept.

She didn't respond. At least the man was talking.

They quickly saddled their horses and rode out of the barn. The three of them went down toward the river. Zach headed north while Tyler and Beth went south. Tyler looked for signs of a boy and dog. Beth recognized what he was doing and forded the river and searched the other side.

They worked in silence and Beth continued to pray they would pick up Riley's trail and find him.

After two hours, they paused. Beth joined Tyler on the other side of the river. Dismounting, Beth pulled the saddlebags off Brownie and led the little horse down to the river for a cool drink.

After Brownie finished, Beth fed the little mare one of the apples she brought. After feeding Brownie, Beth walked around. Tyler stood by the piñon pine tree.

She wanted to reach out to him, but knew he wouldn't welcome her approach. She pulled a second apple from the saddlebags and offered it to Tyler.

"You need to eat something."

He looked at the apple. He started to turn away, but thought better and took the apple. "Thanks."

"I have a Thermos of coffee if you want some."

He didn't reply, but she pulled the Thermos and poured herself some coffee. She settled on a large boulder and sipped the strong brew. She grabbed one of the fruit bars she'd stashed in the saddlebags.

Tyler looked out over the landscape as he finished his apple. Taking the core, he flung it as far away as he could. Beth started to say something to Tyler, but the walkie-talkie squawked.

"There are signs of the boy north of Mesa Road. It looks like he came through here probably ten hours ago."

Sheriff Joe answered the searchers. "We'll send more people to work the north side of the road." The sheriff paused, then came on again. "Zach, you find any signs?"

"None here by the river. Tyler, you got anything?

"No," Tyler answered.

"Okay, with those tracks, why don't you and Beth search south of the road by where the other signs were found."

"Beth and I are on it."

Beth capped the coffee and put it in her saddlebags, then mounted Brownie and followed Tyler north.

* * *

Riley sat on the ground. There was no water and no food anywhere. The mountainous area around the ranch made seeing over the next hill hard. When he reached the top of one hill, all he saw was more hills and rocks. He didn't see a house or a road. When he woke this morning, the sky had been clouded over, so he couldn't use the sun to guide him in walking, but that wouldn't matter, because he didn't know which direction to walk.

His stomach had stopped cramping several hours ago. Now, what he really needed was some water. Looking at the dark clouds, he prayed it would rain, but how would he catch any of it?

"Okay, Dogger, you got any ideas on which way to go?"

Dogger's tongue hung out and he panted. Dogger needed water, too.

"Well, guy, I'm going to let you take the lead. You might do better than me." Riley stood and motioned the dog to go first. Dogger stood and didn't hesitate, but took off. Riley followed.

Several hours later, lightning flashed and the ground shook with the boom of thunder. The sky opened up.

Riley stood there and lifted his face to the sky and opened his mouth. It wasn't enough, so he cupped his hands and caught enough water and lapped it up. After several handfuls of water, he glanced at Dogger.

He cupped his hands again and knelt, offering the water to the dog. Dogger lapped it up.

There wasn't any shelter that they could run to. Instead, Riley sat down and rested his head on his upraised knees. Dogger settled at his side as they waited for the rain to stop.

As they searched for Riley, Tyler tried to keep the guilt at bay. He focused strictly on finding Riley. He didn't want to think about what would happen if they couldn't find the boy, because he knew he couldn't live with his part in driving him away.

"We need to rest the horses," Beth called out.

Tyler didn't want to, but he wouldn't abuse his horse because of his guilt. He reined in and dismounted. He pulled out an apple from his saddle-bags and fed it to his mount.

Beth walked around and stretched her legs. She didn't say anything to him. Instead, she stood still, scanning the horizon. "Lord, lead us in the right direction to find Riley. Keep him safe, no matter where he is."

A streak of lightning raced across the sky, followed by the rattling of the thunder. The horses shied.

"Easy, girl," Beth soothed Brownie.

The rain followed as if someone turned on a showerhead. Beth searched through her saddle-bags for her baseball hat. Tyler readjusted his cowboy hat. There was no shelter closeby, no way to avoid being drenched.

Tyler thought that his relationship with God had begun to heal, but it seemed like everything was working against him.

Try again, a voice inside him whispered.

Could he? Could he trust again?

Lord, I need Your help, because I am lost here. I'm going to trust You. Help us find Riley, well and whole.

The rain stopped as suddenly as it had begun. Maybe there was hope.

Chapter Fourteen

Beth and Tyler returned to the barn close to seven in the evening, soaked to the skin. Although the rain at noon had only lasted a short time, it washed out any tracks Riley might have left. But Tyler and Beth didn't give up. They continued to search. The afternoon had been sunny, but toward the end of the day it had turned cloudy again and the air smelled of the coming rain.

None of the searchers found any further signs of Riley after the rain. Around five in the afternoon, several of the ranchers radioed they were suspending their search to go home and care for their own stock, but promised to resume the search tomorrow.

Sophie and several of the wives who stayed had fixed a dinner for the remaining searchers. As Beth and Tyler walked to the house, the sky opened up again and the rain came down in sheets.

They raced to the porch, rain drenching them to the skin. They were the last two to come in. Beth paused and looked out into the darkened sky.

"Lord, keep him safe," she whispered.

Her words caused Tyler to stop. Bowing his head, he remained motionless for an instant, then walked inside. The room fell silent at their entrance.

Sophie left the living room and reappeared with two towels. Handing one to Tyler, she gave the other one to Beth.

"Thanks." Tyler rubbed his face and hair.

Beth covered her head with the towel. "I'll be back in a few minutes." She disappeared down the hall.

People began to talk again and Zach pulled Tyler to the kitchen table. "Eat. You won't do anyone any good if you pass out."

A pot of chili sat on the stove. The pan of cornbread was on the neighboring burner. It smelled wonderful. Tyler looked at it, wondering if he could eat. Sophie didn't wait for him but dished up two bowls of chili and handed him a bowl.

"Go and eat," Sophie commanded, using her Army voice.

No one moved.

Part of Tyler instantly responded to Sophie's command voice. "What was your rank?" he asked.

"I outranked you, soldier. And as a medic, I

learned not to put up with nonsense. Eat. That's what your body needs, and I think you'll need it for later."

Grabbing a piece of cornbread, Tyler moved to the table. As he passed Zach, he whispered, "I'm impressed."

"You'll thank her later."

Tyler settled at the table and let the crowd around him resume their chatter. Heaven knew there was nothing left in him to engage in conversation, and no one tried.

Riley watched Dogger trot along. The dog would stop every few yards and make sure Riley followed. "Okay, okay, I'm coming," Riley grumbled as he followed behind. He sure prayed the dog knew where he was going, because if he didn't... Up one hill, down another.

Riley refused to think about it.

Dogger disappeared over the ridge of the land. When Riley topped the ridge he saw the stables at Second Chance Ranch in the distance. Excitement raced through Riley's veins. Dogger had done it.

Riley hurried down the other side of the rise and splashed through the shallow stream running at the base and walked up the other side. The dog waited for him. On unsteady legs, Riley tried to climb up the slope. He slipped a couple of times on damp soil and plants, grabbing a few of the scrub bushes on the hill. It took a couple of tries for him to get up the hill.

Once at the top, he could see the parking lot and saw several trucks with their horse trailers leaving the back parking lot.

Looking over the ranch building, Riley saw several police cruisers parked in the drive in front of the main house. Fear snaked up Riley's spine. Had they been looking for him? Now that his panic subsided, Riley realized how much trouble he'd caused and would be in. His courage faltered.

He waited and watched until all the cars left. Once the last police car pulled away, he crept up to the stables. He paused at the treat barrel, grabbed one of the carrots used for rewards for the horses, and took a big bite. It tasted a little dirty, but it was food. He slipped into the stables, wondering what he should do. He turned on the hose used to wash the horses and had a drink of water and washed off the carrot. Dogger lapped up the water on the concrete. Riley let the water run a few moments for the dog to get a drink.

After turning off the water, he wondered what would do now? He heard Charming whinny and he walked to his stall. The horse nodded his head and snatched the carrot from the youth's hand. "Hey, guy. That wasn't for you."

Charming raised his head.

Riley walked over to the reward barrel kept

inside and grabbed another carrot, washed it and started to eat it. He went back to Charming's stall and let himself inside. Sitting in the corner, he wondered what he should do.

Now that the fear had begun to recede, his heart ached from what he'd heard Tyler say. What did he mean?

Leaning against the wooden wall, Riley closed his eyes. His last thought before sleep engulfed him was he was glad to be at the ranch. Dogger had done a good job.

All the searchers had left. Trucks and horse trailers had all cleared out close to an hour ago. Zach sat with Tyler.

"At light, we'll resume the search."

As if his control had finally snapped, Tyler jumped to his feet. "He shouldn't be out there. It's my fault."

"No, it's not," Sophie answered.

"I couldn't save Paul and now I've driven away his younger brother and he could be hurt or dead out in the desert. How could I be so stupid? And Susan, if she hadn't been—"

Beth shot out of her chair and came face to face with him, her outrage making her shake. "I can't believe my ears, Tyler Lynch."

He froze.

"Did you also cause it to rain today, and did you make the sun go down?"

Pulling back, he said, "What are you talking about?"

"Well, since you've elevated yourself to the status of God, can you control the weather, too? Or stop a boy from hearing? Or stop a bomb from exploding by looking at it?"

"You're not making any sense."

"Me. Me. I'm not making sense." Beth saw out of the corner of her eye Zach and Sophie sitting at the kitchen table in stunned disbelief.

"How much sense does it make to think you could've stopped that bomb from exploding and killing Paul? Did you let it explode on purpose?" she demanded.

"That's crazy."

"Exactly, so why are you blaming yourself for the bomb going off? How much sense does that make?"

Tyler simply stared at her. "I should've been the one who died."

Tears rolled down Beth's cheeks. "But you weren't. And I don't know why Paul died, and you didn't, but you lived." She drew a shaky breath.

"Lived. Don't you think that there was a reason? Are you going to be the man who touches Riley's life or are you going to retreat into yourself, beat yourself up emotionally and benefit no one? You don't have the powers to make the wind blow or the earth turn or a bomb not go off. But you *do* have the power to yield to God and have Him direct your footsteps. Neither Susan nor Riley needs your self-flagellation. They need a man who can support them, help them and pray for them. Not someone who's wallowing in self-pity."

"Beth." Zach stood. "That's enough."

She looked at her brother, then Tyler. Her chin trembled. Turning, she raced out of the house.

Anger throbbed through her body. Why couldn't Tyler see that Paul's death was a terrible thing, but it wasn't his fault? How could he be so myopic? All he could see was his pain, crowding out others.

Her emotions driving her, she flew down the steps and headed toward the stables. Halfway there, she doubled over in pain. She couldn't stand by and watch Tyler blame himself for something he had no control over. And Riley, where was he?

She straightened and walked to the first fenced corral. Stopping, she grabbed the top cross post and looked out in to the night. The clouds had cleared and the stars twinkled brightly. The temperature was still in the seventies. Everything looked so clean and renewed.

Resting her head on her hand, she tried to pray, but no words came.

She'd tried so hard to help Riley and Tyler, so

why had it fallen so flat? In the stillness, she tried to find a clue to what had gone wrong. Had she been guilty of trying to manage this situation with Riley and Tyler in her own strength instead of letting God work His perfect timing?

Was she trying to do God's job as Tyler was?

Yes.

The stunning truth robbed her knees of strength, and she stumbled over to Riley's bench by the stable door. Her heart told her that she'd tried to orchestra Riley's and Tyler's lives and not let God do it His way. She thought she knew what was best for everyone and—

She went still.

Was she the problem here, not Tyler? Was getting Tyler to talk a prime example of trying to direct someone's life instead of allowing God to work His way? Her stomach sank.

The last time she thought she could change someone's life was with her boyfriend in high school. When she finally realized he was controlling, she thought she could change him with her sunny smile and gentle coaxing. How well had that gone?

And what had her reaction been to that disaster? She'd closed her heart, not allowing any male to get too close.

Now, finally, she'd opened her heart and fallen in love and done what?

Love.

She could admit it now. She loved Tyler. She'd let a man inside her heart and what had she done? Messed up.

She wanted to laugh hysterically.

Lord, I finally opened my heart and I drive him away.

Well, wasn't she clever? She'd fallen in love with a man who'd decided to lock himself away again. Leaning against the stable, she closed her eyes and let the pain wash over her.

Tyler stood in the living room, staring at the screen door where Beth had just stormed out. His ears still rang from her tirade.

Zach came to Tyler's side. "She didn't mean it. Beth just sometimes gets wound up. I've been on the wrong end of her tongue lashing before."

Tyler ran his fingers through his hair. "Yeah, she sure can tear a strip off a guy." But his spirit told him Beth had nailed it. He turned to Sophie, who sat at the table but hadn't offered any comment. "You agree with your husband?"

She remained quiet for a few moments. "What happened in Iraq?"

"Sophie," Zach protested.

Tyler held up his hand. "Your wife's right." He walked to the table and explained to them about the call to disarm the bomb and what had happened in that café.

Sophie's fingers played with the remains of her shredded napkin. "I've seen soldiers blame themselves when their buddies die, wanting to go back and be the one who was killed. But you were wounded, as well, not only physically, but mentally. And if I don't miss my guess, spiritually. Beth's right, Tyler. Paul's death wasn't your fault, but only you can decide to let go of that poison."

The truth kept hitting him over the head.

Zach glared at his wife. Ignoring her comment, he explained, "Beth tends to get into everyone's business."

Tyler gave a short bark of laughter. "I know."

"Like she did for you when she dragged you here?" Sophie replied to her husband.

Zach frowned.

"I see your point, Sophie," Tyler inserted, trying to avoid the coming fight. "I'll think about what she said."

Sophie leaned in. "I've never known Beth to be cruel and try to hurt someone. Her heart's desire is to help others. She carried Zach's pain—" Sophie's voice got thick "—and my pain when we couldn't see beyond our noses. I know her, and she's acting from concern for you and Riley. Please keep that in mind."

"I will." He left, wanting to think about Beth

and Sophie's words, because deep down in his heart he knew he heard the truth.

Beth heard a dog bark, pulling her out of her despair. Opening her eyes, she looked down and saw Dogger.

"Hey, guy, where have you been?" She bent down to pet him, but the dog stood and walked to the open double doors. When she didn't follow him, too involved with her self-pity, Dogger came back and sat down before her and waited.

"What?"

He stood and went to the door.

"Okay, boy." Standing, she followed him into the stables. It suddenly dawned on her that Dogger had gone with Riley.

Her heart pounding, she followed the dog to Charming's stall. Beth approached the stall carefully, wondering what she would see.

She moved to the stall door and looked inside. Curled in the corner was Riley. By his hand was a partially eaten carrot, one of the ones they kept for the horses. "Oh, Dogger, you did such a good job."

She debated whether to wake Riley up or run and get Tyler. She turned and ran out of the stables and saw Tyler on the walk between the houses. She motioned for him to come. When he started out slowly, she motioned for him to hurry.

"What is it?"

"Riley's in Charming's stall. He's asleep."

As if shot out of a cannon, Tyler darted into the stables. He came to a stop in front of Charming's stall. He looked at the boy curled in the corner. "How did you find him?"

"It wasn't me. Dogger came to me when I was outside on the bench and dragged me in here."

The dog stood at their feet, looking up as if to say, "I did my job." Tyler knelt and rubbed the dog's throat. "You haven't failed me yet, friend."

His words pierced Beth's soul.

Standing, he released the lever on the door and walked into the stall. Charming started to dance. Beth raced in and crooned to the horse, settling him down. Tyler scooped the boy into his arms. He bowed his head as if giving thanks, then walked out of the stall.

"Are his clothes wet?" Beth asked.

"A little." He walked out and headed for the doors. Dogger trailed along behind Tyler. Beth closed Charming in and followed behind them. She rushed in front of Tyler and opened the door of the foreman's house. Tyler placed the boy on the sofa.

Riley's eyes fluttered open. When he saw Tyler's face, Riley sat up. Riley looked at Beth, then at Tyler. "Did you kill my brother?"

The simple, direct question made tears roll

down Beth's cheeks. She prayed for Tyler that he could answer Riley. And prayed for grace that Riley could hear and accept the truth.

And not judge.

Tyler knew his next few words would be some of the most important of his life. When Beth had torn into him earlier, it was as if someone had slapped him in the face, waking him up. No matter how hard he wanted to, he couldn't change what happened to Paul. He'd tried to save his friend, but it had not turned out that way. He was alive and Paul wasn't. He couldn't save Paul, but he could save Riley.

"No, I didn't kill your brother." They were the hardest words he would ever utter.

"Then why did you tell Beth it was your fault?" His young eyes pierced to the very core of Tyler's soul.

"Your brother and I were trying to disarm a bomb. I had turned away when it exploded." He couldn't describe what the bomb had physically done to his friend. "It killed Paul. I got a few scratches." Tyler grasped Riley's hand. "I wish it would've been me instead of your brother, but it wasn't."

Moisture filled the boy's eyes. "So you're trying to be my friend because you feel guilty?"

The verbal blow hit Tyler square between the

eyes. "I wanted to visit and tell both your mother and you what a fine man Paul was. When I got home from Iraq, I visited your old home and discovered you'd moved. I got your new address from the neighbors. I traveled around the country for a while and I finally worked up the courage to come here to talk to your mom. I ran into Zach and he offered me the job here at the ranch.

"But what I thought would just be an apology turned into something much more. I discovered I enjoyed talking to you and your mom. She asked me to bring you out here. I rediscovered how much I liked working with horses and the ranching life. It connected me with my early years when my parents were still alive.

"I think that Paul would've liked it if we were friends. I know I could never replace Paul, and I wouldn't even try. But maybe I could be an honorary big brother to you and if you had any questions about school or girls, I could answer. We could go riding and if you like fishing, maybe we could do that. You know, your mom's going to need a lot of help when she gets out of the hospital. I want to be there to help. Could I do that?"

Riley studied him and his mouth curved into a shy smile. "Okay."

Tyler offered Riley his hand. The boy accepted it, then threw himself onto Tyler's chest.

Tyler's arms encircled the youth, his relief making him giddy. The warmth of Beth's hand on his shoulder added to his contentment. She reached over his shoulder and stroked Riley's head. Dogger rested his paws on Tyler's lap.

"Welcome home," she whispered, and Tyler wondered who she was speaking to.

Riley pulled back. "I'm hungry. And I know Dogger is, too."

Beth laughed, and Riley grinned back.

"There wasn't anything out there to eat."

"Where were you?" Beth asked.

Riley looked down at his hands and lifted one shoulder. "Don't know." He raised his head. "After I heard Tyler, I just shot out of the barn and started running. I stumbled a couple of times, but kept running until I got a stitch in my side. After a while, I was so lost. That's when Dogger found me." He reached down and petted the dog's head. "I don't know how he found me, but I was so glad he showed up. He made me feel better.

"I thought I'd find a road and could hitch a ride to the hospital or something, but I didn't come across anything."

"Where were you last night?" Beth asked.

Riley looked at Tyler and then Beth. "I found a rock, and Dogger and I huddled close to it. Today, I finally let Dogger lead the way." He leaned down and hugged the dog. "And he brought me home."

Dogger lifted his head and enjoyed all the

scratches and praises he received. Riley laughed at the dog's antics.

"Well, there's chili and cornbread up at the main house. Does that sound good to you?" Beth asked.

"Yup." Riley shot out of the stable, leaving Beth and Tyler staring at the empty door.

Chapter Fifteen

Riley raced down the hall to his mother's hospital room and stopped short inside the door. His eyes went wide at the sight of her. Both her legs were in traction and her head was bandaged. He glanced over his shoulder at Beth and Tyler.

Beth wrapped her arm around his shoulders. "Your mom's out of ICU and the doctors felt she was strong enough to be in this room. They wouldn't have put her here if they were worried. And no matter what she looks like, she's doing well."

He looked to Tyler as if for reassurance.

"She's right. They moved her last night." He didn't need to add, when they were looking for him.

Riley walked to his mother's bed. "Can I touch her?"

"I don't see why not." Beth sent him a smile of encouragement.

Carefully, he stepped to the bed. "Mom." He touched her right arm.

Susan's eyes fluttered open. "Hey," came her whispered reply. She licked her lips. "Water."

Looking around, Riley found a cup with a straw in it. He picked it up.

"Go ahead," Beth encouraged.

He held the cup so his mother could sip the water. Susan took a couple of sips. She collapsed back onto her pillow.

Riley clasped his mother's hand. "I was afraid I'd lose you."

Susan tried to smile, but the bruises on her face made her wince. "I'm going to be all right, son. It's going to take a little time, but I'll be okay." She looked at Tyler and Beth.

Tyler moved next to Riley. "You don't worry, Susan. I'll take care of Riley. Until you're out of the hospital, he can stay with me, and afterward, we'll work something out."

"Thank you. I don't know what I would've done if—"

"I'm here for you." Tyler rested his hand on her arm. "And I'm sure I speak for Beth, too."

Beth walked around to the other side of the bed, facing Riley and Tyler. "Of course you can count on me. No matter what you need, we'll help."

Tears gathered in Susan's eyes. "Thank you."

Tyler looked uncomfortable with her gratitude.

Susan closed her eyes.

The door opened and the doctor entered.

"Ah, her family is here." After introductions were made, the doctor checked out his patient. "You're looking good, Susan."

She looked down at her legs. "Really."

"Really. When we can set those legs, we will, but the critical time has passed. Now, it's letting your body recover." He explained to all what the next few months would entail.

"What about work?" she asked.

"You might not be able to get into work, but I don't see why you can't do it over the phone and internet." The doctor turned to the group. "Guys, keep the visit short. She needs her rest." With those words, he left.

Beth started for the door.

"Can I sit here for a couple of minutes with Mom?" Riley asked.

"Of course. Beth and I will be in the waiting room across from the nurses' station."

They walked down the hall to the waiting area across from the nurses' station. Beth felt embarrassed by her earlier rant at Tyler. She wanted to tell him she was sorry, but another couple sat down.

Riley soon appeared in the waiting area and they drove Beth back to her car, which was still parked at the church. Beth quickly said her goodbyes, escaped the car and headed home. Her heart was still in turmoil. Tyler and Riley had come to a tentative peace which, on one hand, made her heart sing, but if she thought about Tyler, her heart was at war with itself.

Had she blown it with him?

She didn't know, but her words, while true, weren't easy for him to hear. Beth wanted to pick up the phone and talk to Tyler, but her courage failed her.

She'd call him tomorrow.

Several days later when David called Beth's office, Beth knew she had the excuse she needed to escape Albuquerque. She convinced her boss she needed to go to Tuba City.

When she walked into David's studio, he frowned. "What are you doing here, *querida?*" He stood and walked around his massive desk.

"You had a problem."

"Which we resolved over the phone." He wrapped his arm around her shoulders and guided her over to a bench on the patio off his studio/ office. "What is breaking that beautiful heart?"

Beth's eyes watered and a tear escaped. She'd been miserable all week. After she got over her embarrassment about yelling at Tyler, she had to admit that she'd fallen in love. And although he was nothing like her high school flame, knowing she was in love made her nervous.

Could she risk her heart again? Could Tyler forgive her for pushing him to admit his issues and for Riley overhearing it?

God had gotten hold of her, letting her know that His timing was perfect and she didn't know exactly when that timing was. It was painful to see how she'd pushed and pulled and rushed into things.

"I think I may have been too quick to reject your overtures."

David frowned. "You are a terrible liar, *querida,* which makes me very happy, since I'll always know if you are telling me the truth when we do business. But for you, that is not good. What has caused you this pain—or who?"

"Oh, David, I blew it. I've finally fallen in love and just yelled at the man for feeling guilty about something he can't change."

Frowning, David asked, "Why did you do this?"

Beth explained what had happened.

"Do you want me to go to Albuquerque and beat this man to a pulp?"

Beth laughed into her tissue.

"Ah, a smile."

"No, David, I don't want you to do that."

He picked up her hand and held it. "It seems to

me that it would be wrong for you to give up on this young man. I've noticed a difference in you, *querida*. I thought it was me who brought that smile, but I am not so vain to think another man could make your heart sing.

"You spoke the truth to me about my art always being first in my heart. I will return the favor. Your heart is speaking to you. Do not ignore it."

Beth realized David had revealed his heart to her, and his words of advice weren't fluff, but heartfelt words.

She hugged his arm. "Thank you, David, for being a true friend."

He grinned. "And if you need me to come and challenge this man, call me. I will come."

Beth laughed and for the first time felt hope.

When Beth got back to her apartment, she found Ethan sitting on the steps leading to her apartment.

"What are you doing here?" Beth asked.

"I came to see why you are hiding."

"Oh." She walked past him and unlocked her apartment door. Ethan followed.

"You're not going to deny it?"

Putting her purse on the kitchen counter, she turned to face her brother. "No. And if you're going to rake me over the coals, take a number."

Her brother's eyes narrowed. "What does that mean?"

"It means that I've already been told I can't solve my problems by running away."

"Who did that?" he asked in a brotherly tone. She didn't doubt he would challenge whoever had talked to her.

"One of my clients. He told me, politely, I can't run away from my heart. Are you going to tell me the same thing?"

Ethan's surprised expression made Beth laugh. "Did I steal your thunder?"

He pulled her into his arms. "Yeah. We've had to beg and stand on our heads to get people to cover for you at the ranch. I've spent more time with Zach than I want to," he teased. "I also spent time with a very sad Tyler and Riley. Riley keeps asking where you are and Tyler doesn't have a good answer."

Shame for her actions filled Beth. She tipped her head up and smiled at Ethan. "Thank you, big brother. I need to go fix the problem."

Tyler drove back from the high school where Riley was attending his first day of school. Oddly, the first day fell on a Wednesday. He stopped by the counseling office and explained to the counselors the situation with Riley and gave them his information. As he left, a sense of purpose filled his heart.

The gaping wound left by Paul's death had begun to heal. The scar would always be there, but he knew there was hope. And a new purpose in his life. The person who'd made him face his demons had removed herself from his life. Hearing her say it wasn't his fault, that he couldn't control the situation made him realize that he was blaming himself for something he couldn't control. Once he'd been freed of the guilt, the sun had started shining again.

Thanks to Beth.

A woman who made herself scarce.

He knew she'd dropped by the hospital and talked with Susan, but she hadn't been back to the ranch. Arrangements had been made for other volunteers to fill in for her. Her excuse was that she had a sudden business trip. He'd asked Sophie about it. She'd confirmed Beth was out of town. He wanted to believe that's what happened, but there was something nagging him.

He worried over it. He missed her sunny face and joyful laugh. He and Riley had prayed every night for his mother's healing and read a scripture together. He even called his parents again. He asked his mother how to help Riley as she'd helped him. She tried not to cry, but he heard the emotion filling her voice. He made peace with his family. His foster mother told him that his ex-fiancée had married two weeks after he left and quickly divorced two months later.

They also wanted to come out to the ranch and visit in late September.

And he made peace with God. That first night Riley had spent at his home, he stood at the door-way looking at the boy. He asked God to forgive him. A sense of peace had flowed over him. The first thing he wanted to do was tell Beth, but she hadn't come anywhere near him.

Parking his truck, he walked to the stables and started his chores. As he worked in the feed room, Ollie appeared.

"You in a better mood this morning?"

The words startled Tyler, stopping him. "What are you talking about?"

"You've been stomping around here like a wounded bull. I'm surprised you haven't run off clients and sent Riley screaming from the ranch."

This was Mr. Grumpy calling him out. "What are you talking about?"

"I've seen wounded bulls with less attitude than you."

No words came to Tyler's mind.

"With the looks you and Miss Beth were throw-ing at each other over the last month, I'm sur-prised you didn't catch these stables on fire. Now, Missy's not coming around, making lame excuses and sending substitutes. Something ain't right between you two. Fix it." He stomped out.

Tyler could only stare in amazement at the open door. The man known for his bad attitude chewed him out for a bad attitude. It really must stink.

He shook his head and went back to work. A few minutes later, Zach appeared.

"You okay? Or did Ollie tear a strip off you?"

Finished with his work, Tyler walked out of the feed room. "Well, I'll say he didn't mince words."

"Good."

The statement knocked Tyler back on his heels. "What are you talking about? Why's Ollie chewing me out good?"

"You know that Ollie was on chemo for cancer. He's had a rough six months. He worked through it. He'd come here and puke his guts out, but that never stopped him. He was nice to folks."

"How's that bad?"

"Because it wasn't our Ollie, with a tart tongue and straight answers. He's the one who told me that riding talent wasn't in my lost leg. Slapped me up the side of the head, letting me know I was wallowing in self-pity. Lately, he's been his old ornery self, which is good news. Sophie's overjoyed with his old attitude. I am, too, even if it is hard to hear sometimes."

At his expense. "It's nice to know there's a silver lining in the situation."

Zach slapped him on the back. "I wouldn't worry about Beth. I think she's embarrassed that she blew up and said what she did. Now I think she doesn't know how to fix it. She might need a little encouragement from you."

Hope filled his heart. "You think?"

"I know. My sister sometimes lets her mouth run before engaging her brain." Zach rubbed his neck. "Unfortunately, even then, she's usually right. Doesn't that just make you want to grind your teeth when that happens?"

Smiling, Tyler shook his head. "She certainly set me straight." More like yanking a knot in his tail. They moved down the walk toward the parking lot.

Zach winced. "She—"

Putting up his hand to stop Zach, Tyler shook his head. "I'm not mad. In fact, I'm grateful that she took me to task." Life certainly looked better, except for missing her. "I just wish she'd show up again, so I could talk to her."

"She's got a phone. A cell, too."

Laughter shook Tyler's chest. "Give me her number."

Zach rattled off the numbers. "You might think about getting a cell phone, yourself. You're going to need that phone closeby if you've got Riley and Susan needing to talk to you."

He hadn't considered that idea, but Tyler knew

it was time. "I think Riley might like to help me pick it out. I'm off to pick him up and take him to the hospital."

"Good luck."

He didn't need it. He had God on his side.

"That's way cool," Riley said. He looked at the cell phone that Tyler had just bought. "I'll have to program your new number into my cell. So you goin' to call Beth, to see where she is?"

Tyler pulled away from the cell phone store and headed toward the hospital. "You miss Beth?"

"Yeah, how come she's been gone all week? Did you have a fight with her?"

Had he worn his feelings on the sleeve? Apparently the entire world knew how he felt about Beth. Why hadn't someone told him? "What makes you say that?"

Riley snorted.

"Dumb question, huh?"

"Yeah. Both you and Beth got goofy looks on your faces when you looked at each other. It was real plain." Riley stared out the passenger-side window. "You going to fix it?"

Okay, Father, I get the message. I'll talk to her. "I am. I promise I'll talk with her today."

"You going to tell her you love her?"

"I am."

"Finally."

* * *

Beth stood by the head of Susan's bed. She'd wanted to see Susan before she walked into the lion's den. Susan's bruises had reached their peak of color.

"I'm looking bad," Susan muttered through her swollen lips."

"True, but it's really a good thing. It means you're healing."

Susan's eyes meet Beth's. Susan tried to laugh, but winced at the pain. "Don't make me laugh." Her hand crawled across the sheets and grabbed Beth's. "What's wrong?"

"Why would you ask that?"

"I have broken legs, ribs, but I'm not blind. You haven't been here with Tyler or Riley."

Beth couldn't keep eye contact with Susan. "Tyler and I, well, we sort of had a falling out."

"A lovers' spat?"

"I wish." Beth couldn't tell Susan the guilt riding Tyler.

"Riley told me about hearing what Tyler said."

Beth's eyes widened. "He did, and Tyler and I talked." Susan's mouth trembled. "I told him he wasn't the person responsible for what happened."

Beth could only gape at Susan.

"Don't walk away from Tyler, Beth. I like seeing him smile, and I think you are the reason for his smiles."

Hope shined in her misery. Beth grasped Susan's hand. "Thank you."

The door opened and Riley barreled into the room. "Hey, Mom. Beth, you're here." He threw himself at Beth and hugged her. "I missed seeing you this week."

His actions so startled Beth that for a moment she froze. Tyler stood in the doorway, looking too tall and too handsome.

Shaking off her stupor, she hugged Riley. "How are you?"

"I'm great and have lots of news about school and the new volunteers from the church youth group and the new riders I helped, but you haven't been by the ranch, so how could I tell you?"

Guilt shot through her.

"And you know what," Riley continued, "Tyler just got a new cell phone so he could call you. And I helped him pick it out. It's just way too cool."

Beth's gaze flew to Tyler's. He smiled and shrugged.

"Mom, how are you today? I've got lots of stuff to tell to you. School is so cool. I was telling kids about the ranch and everyone is interested and wants to come out and volunteer. We have to do community hours and several of the kids in my class want to come to Second Chance."

Beth moved away from the bed to allow mother and son to talk. Tyler motioned for her to follow him.

She glanced over her shoulder at the two talking. Before she could move or decide anything, Tyler took her hand and led her into the hall. He didn't stop but walked to the stairwell and opened the door.

The moment the door closed, he turned, cupped her face and kissed her, knocking her socks off.

Stunned, Beth remained still for a millisecond, then returned his kiss. When he drew back, his eyes were dark with passion.

"Thank you, Beth McClure, for taking me to task. You hit the nail on the head. I was wallowing in self-pity."

She opened her mouth to object, but he laid a finger over her lips.

"I was being selfish. All I can say is Paul's death knocked the foundation out from under me. I turned my back on God. But He sent this little ray of sunshine into my darkness, and she wouldn't take no for an answer. She made me face those ugly memories and managed to get me back to church." He rested his forehead against hers.

"I shouldn't have yelled at you," she explained. "That little speech I gave you was as much for me as it was for you. I realized that I was holding on to a past bad relationship."

He pushed back several strands of her hair that had fallen on her face. "Have anything to do with that showdown Riley and I witnessed at your store?"

"How did you know?"

His brow arched. "If looks could kill, that guy would've been laid out there on the men's department floor."

Beth blushed.

"Want to tell me about it?"

She remained quiet.

"I've discovered confronting those demons is better than hiding from them."

She couldn't refuse to tell him when he'd opened his heart to her. "Okay."

She opened her mouth, but he held up his hand. He pulled her toward the steps and sat down, patting the area beside him.

She settled by his side.

"Now, talk to me."

She took a deep steadying breath, launching into her explanation, "The man you saw was Gavin Humphrey. He was star quarterback and my boyfriend my senior year. Every girl in our high school drooled over him—"

"Really?"

He looked so puzzled that Beth had to laugh.

"You had to be there. Now, where was I? Oh, when Gavin asked me to homecoming, I was the envy of all the girls, and not just the seniors, but every female in that school."

He shook his head.

"After I got over my starry-eyed rush, I discovered Gavin was a control freak. He tried to control all the things in my life. He was very clever and didn't ever say anything in public that would warn others, but when we were in private, he'd tell me he didn't like this person or I shouldn't associate with another person. If I wore something he didn't like, he'd tell me about it. Didn't I know those stripes made me look fat? I had a green sweater that he hated and he told me not to wear it. The second time I wore it, it accidentally got caught in the car door and dragged all over town.

"I didn't want to tell my parents and I couldn't tell my brothers, because I know they would've gone after him. I convinced myself just to endure until the summer. Gavin was going to a different college than me. When I bucked him after the senior prom, not leaving when he wanted to go, he slapped me."

Tyler's eyes flamed with anger.

She held up her hand. "I never saw him again after that night."

"That's what Kelly meant," Tyler whispered.

"What?"

"Kelly warned me, along with Pastor Mike, not to hurt you."

Beth nodded.

"What happened with Gavin?"

"I never saw the man again until the other day in the store. He called after his summer vacation, but I never accepted his calls. He never got close enough to me to hurt me again.

"After Gavin, I haven't let any man close to me, that is, until you came along. I ran into this cautious dog and his equally cautious owner. I was instantly intrigued. How could I know you used your dog to reel me in?"

"So does that mean you love me?" Hope filled Tyler's dark eyes.

"Yes."

"Then you might consider getting married."

"I don't understand."

Rubbing the back of his neck, he shook his head. "I'm making a mess of this. I love you, Beth McClure, and I want to spend the rest of my life with you. Will you marry me?"

Her heart swelled in her chest. This amazing man cared so much for his friend that the grief nearly killed him. But he was faithful to his friend, trying to help a family that wasn't his. No matter, through thick and thin, he'd been there. He never demanded perfection, or criticized anything anyone did, which was the main fear of her heart.

She threw her arms around his neck. "Of course I'll marry you."

Applause rang in the stairwell, followed by a good job and congratulations. Riley opened the stair door and grinned.

"'bout time."

They laughed.

"Let's go back inside and tell your mother the good news," Tyler urged.

Beth's eye glistened with happiness. "Let's do it."

Tyler opened the door, and led them back to Susan's room and a new life.

Epilogue

Tyler looked around the large dinner table set for a big Easter luncheon. After attending the sunrise service, they went back to the ranch to get ready for the meal. He stepped up behind Beth, slid his arms around her waist and kissed her cheek.

"Happy Easter, Mrs. Lynch."

She rested her hands over his. "It is a blessed Easter."

He buried his face in her neck.

"Hey, you two, stop that," Zack protested. "You've got kids in the room." He held in his arms his two-month old son. "Ignore them, Adam. They're newlyweds and dumb."

"Oh, the perils of fatherhood." Beth laughed. "Let me have that little one." She walked out of Tyler's arms and took the baby from her brother. "Why don't you help your wife with dinner? Company will be here soon." Beth headed for the living room, cooing and talking nonsense to the baby.

The changes in Tyler's life still startled him. Beth had filled his days with laughter and aggravation. She got him to talk about his parents, his grandmother and the painful years of wandering from foster home to foster home. She gave him a new guitar for a wedding present and had encouraged him to play for her.

He missed her the days she traveled for her job. He still worked here on the ranch, but the city of Albuquerque had a job opening in the police department. They needed men to work in the bomb disposal unit. He hadn't talked to Beth yet, but he knew his talent was needed there. He'd talked with the guys in the bomb unit, and they were ready for him to go through training so he could join them.

A car stopped outside and he heard the car doors slam shut. Beth's parents were here, but he heard others talking to them. They opened the front door and walked inside.

"Tyler, I've got someone here you might want to see," Lynda McClure called out.

Stepping into the foyer, he saw his foster parents and siblings. He waded into the group and hugged each of them. They had driven to Albuquerque to attend his wedding on the last weekend of January. After the ceremony they'd talked with Tyler about legally adopting him. The notion floored him, and he questioned if they could do such a thing, given his age. Yes, indeed they could. They had the papers and with his permission, they'd file them. His life overflowed with love and blessings.

"What are you doing here?" he asked his mother.

"We've got a court date for the final adoption hearing. I wanted to tell you in person. Besides, we all wanted to visit the ranch again."

He pulled her into his arms, his emotions overflowing. "Thanks."

Another car pulled in, and Tyler heard Riley calling out. "We're here."

Beth appeared in the foyer, holding Adam. The women oohed and aahed over the baby. Tyler opened the door and watched as Riley helped his mother out of the front seat. Her car had been fitted with hand controls, allowing her to drive. Today would be her first therapy lesson.

The dinner table filled with family and friends. As he looked around the table, his heart swelled. Beth slipped her hand in his.

"Amazing, isn't it?" she whispered.

"It is a gift beyond understanding."

Zach tapped his water glass with his fork. "Let's say grace before we eat. Tyler, would you bless the food?"

Everyone held hands.

"Heavenly Father, we thank You for every person here at this table. You have brought us through many trials, but You've always been here for us. Your gifts and grace are beyond understanding. Thank You for your precious Son who gave His life for us. Thank You for this bounty. In Jesus's name."

"Amen," came the united response.

He closed his eyes, letting the Amen wash over him.

His life had been restored.

* * * * *

Dear Reader,

I hope you've enjoyed Beth and Tyler's story. This story was inspired by a TV special, *The Dogs of War*. It was about how the U.S. Army in WWII asked people to volunteer their dogs to be trained to work with the soldiers. It was followed by an update on how several soldiers found dogs in Iraq and brought them home. Those dogs were a comfort to the soldiers. The story grabbed me by the heart.

I knew immediately when Tyler appeared at Second Chance Ranch he would be the hero in Beth's story. Beth is a woman who doesn't believe in defeat, and if things aren't going as she thinks they should, she wants "to help." She learns that only God can heal the heart, no matter how good the intentions are. I hope you enjoyed their story.

Leann Harris

Questions for Discussion

1. What did you think of Dogger introducing Beth and Tyler?

2. What do you think of Tyler's reaction to Dogger wanting Beth to pet him?

3. Tyler is consumed with guilt. Do you think his feelings are rational? Legitimate?

4. Do you know someone who blames themself for a tragedy they couldn't control? How did you handle it? What do you think of the way Beth handled it?

5. What do you think of Tyler reaching out to his buddy's family (the Carters)?

6. What's your opinion on how Beth handles the situation with Riley, not allowing him to pout?

7. Beth accidentally says something that blows up in her face when she asks about Riley's brother. What do you think of her reaction? Has that happened to you? How did you handle it?

8. The all-night lock-in is an experience for Tyler and Riley. Have you gone to a lock-in? As a participant? As the chaperone?

9. Tyler's guilt eats at him. When he confesses it to Beth, Riley overhears. What was your reaction? What do you think of Beth's response to Tyler's feelings?

10. Beth doesn't tactfully handle Tyler's guilt after Riley disappears. What was your reaction to her blurting out the truth? Did she have a point?

11. Tyler's foster family adopts him as an adult. Have you ever heard of that? What do you think of Tyler's reaction?

12. What did you take away from the book?

LARGER-PRINT BOOKS!

GET 2 FREE
LARGER-PRINT NOVELS
PLUS 2 FREE
MYSTERY GIFTS

Love Inspired™

Larger-print novels are now available...

Love Inspired®
SUSPENSE

RIVETING INSPIRATIONAL ROMANCE

Watch for our series of edge-
of-your-seat suspense novels.
These contemporary tales
of intrigue and romance
feature Christian characters
facing challenges to their faith...
and their lives!

AVAILABLE IN REGULAR
& LARGER-PRINT FORMATS

For exciting stories that reflect traditional values,
visit:
www.ReaderService.com